I0537457

THE BARNHART INTRUDER

R. Annan

Copyright 2014 R. Annan

WGAE Reg. # R27870 (09/14/2010)

Printed in the United States of America

Published by One Vision Publishing

Print Book ISBN: 978-1-942338-12-3

EBook ISBN: 978-1-942338-13-0

Dedication

to

My Beloved Angel, Elke

1.

"You wanted to see me, Mr. Davidson, sir?" The accent was American.

"Yes, Robert, come in." The accent was British.

Davidson, Robert Ederly's boss, looked across his desk, watching as the young American closed the door.

"Please sit down," Davidson said. He pointed at some chairs in front of his desk.

Ederly sat in the closest chair facing Davidson. The American had been in Hong Kong for almost two years now, and was content in his nine-to-three job doing paperwork behind a desk down on the lowest floor of the Barnhart Building. He had been out of sight, and out of mind, until now.

Down there he was more or less on his own boss, and often got away early for tennis or golf. All he did was sign shipping manifests for supplies to be sent to the company's enclaves on Banri Island, three hundred miles east, in the South China Sea. The four enclaves on the island purchased artifacts from the natives and shipped them back by boat to

1

the Barnhart warehouses in Hong Kong for worldwide sale and distribution.

"What's up, sir?" Ederly asked.

He brushed his jet-black hair out of his eyes and smiled. He was handsome and he knew it. He also knew the girls in the Barnhart offices knew it. This gave him a false sense of superiority and confidence that the other men at Barnhart disliked. One even called him a hubristic bastard.

"They brought Turner back from the west enclave." Davidson spoke with a distinct lord of the manor accent.

"Oh?" Ederly tried to sound interested. Actually, he wasn't. He didn't know who Turner was. "Did something happen?"

"Delirious...raving mad. Keeps saying, 'they did it...they tried to poison me.'"

"They poisoned him? Who might they be, sir?" Ederly asked.

"Yes, that is the question, isn't it?"

Davidson leaned forward in his swivel chair and took a cigar from the humidor on his desk. After giving it a sniff, and biting off its tip, he stared at it before putting it into his mouth. Finally he took a wooden match from a tin on his desk.

"How would you like to go to the island and sort it out, Robert? See if there is any merit to it. It might be a big fuss over nothing…some sort of accident, perhaps."

Ederly felt uneasy. He coughed and cleared his throat.

"Wouldn't the Banri police be better suited for that, sir?" Ederly looked as if he was about to panic as he watched Davidson light his cigar and blow a cloud of smoke in his direction. "I wouldn't know how to, as you say, sort it out, would I, sir?"

"That's the dilemma, you see, my boy," Davidson continued. "We have to keep this hushed up, Robert…keep it in the family. We can't have the natives butting into our private business and manhandling our people, can we now? The Banri police are a nasty lot. They're as corrupt as the day is long. They're uncivilized as well. You see the problem, don't you, Robert?"

"Well, I…"

"We can't have them snooping into the corporation's private affairs, you know."

3

"I suppose not sir."

"Exactly. So that's why I'm sending you to Banri as Turner's replacement," Davidson said. Ederly expected Davidson to add, "Besides, you're such a boor we don't really need you here…" But he didn't. Instead he said, "Your real job will be to find out just what happened to Turner…to get the facts and report back to me."

Ederly swallowed hard. "As his replacement sir? Do his job?"

"Well, yes…you'll have to do some work, or they'll be on to you, won't they?"

"Ah, couldn't I just go in there and ask questions and all?"

Davidson chuckled. "I'm afraid that wouldn't get you anywhere, Robert. You couldn't just pop in on them and say, 'Which one of you buggers poisoned Turner?'"

"Ah, I suppose not."

"No, of course not." Actually, Ederly didn't see why not, but he didn't have the nerve to argue the point.

"Anyway, perhaps Turner is all wrong. Perhaps he imagined it. After all, he's not in his right mind, what with a high fever and all…but we have to find out what's what." Davidson leaned back in his chair and inhaled and blew a billow of smoke up towards the ceiling fan. "The doctor said I should only smoke two of these a day."

"Are you sure I'm the man for this type of job, sir? I mean…"

"Yes, Robert…you go sort it out. Go on the next supply boat. Sniff it all out." Davidson paused to watch the fan disperse the smoke. "Would you do that for me Robert? As a personal favor?"

Ederly felt trapped. He searched his mind for a viable excuse to get out of it. Before he could come up with one, Davidson came at him again.

"Oh, yes," he said, "Turner also mentioned something about drugs and immoral behavior and strange goings on…dancing with the devil…that sort of thing. You look into all of that, Robert. On the hush. Be discrete. Bring back a full report to me. We don't want to bother old Barnhart with any of this."

Ederly looked down at his white, canvas loafers, as if searching for an escape hatch. Nothing there. He sniffed and stared down his nose, a habit he had developed unconsciously.

"Would you do that for me, Robert?" Davidson repeated. It was more of a command than a request.

Ederly knew that Davidson had him over a barrel. If it wasn't for Davidson, Ederly wouldn't have this plush job. Oh, maybe he'd have a job, alright, but he'd have to work. Ederly didn't like work. When he was a junior officer, a second lieutenant in Korea, he had sat behind a desk in a tech-and-intel outfit, back in Seoul. He read reports and passed them on, and did little else. And, as a special perk, he got to go to Hong Kong for rest and recuperation for a week, where he stayed at a plush hotel and went to the golf course and played tennis.

That's where he met Davidson, at the hotel tennis court. Davidson's partner had to cancel, so Ederly asked if he might step in. Davidson shrugged and said okay. He and his partner rarely won a game anyway, so he had nothing to lose except the ten-pound wager. They won the game and Davidson was so surprised and elated that he took the young lieutenant out to dinner. The next day they won another ten pounds, and two more times after that. The following week,

Davidson took him over to the six-story Barnhart building on the harbor. The Barnhart warehouse and dock were right next door.

He gave Ederly a grand tour of the building. Ederly, looking trim and handsome in his officer's uniform, was the center of attention, especially among the secretaries who wanted to know if he was married. Before the American went back to Seoul, Davidson gave him his card.

"If you need a job when you get out, Lieutenant," Davidson said, "look me up."

At the end of his twelve-month tour, Ederly went home to Rhode Island. He stayed there a while, got bored, and drifted across the country from job to job. One day, in California, he pulled out Davidson's card and stared at it for a long time. A week later he was in Hong Kong, working for his old friend.

But he never expected it would lead to anything like this.

"We figured that since you have a background in army intelligence, you would be perfect for this kind of thing," Davidson said.

7

Ederly wanted desperately to yell out, "But all I did was sit behind a desk and sign papers, sir!" But he couldn't. It would be too embarrassing. Too personal and revealing. After all, he bragged about being in the intelligence field just to sound important and impress the Barnhart secretaries.

Ederly knew, at that point, he was trapped.

"Well, yes, I guess I could do it, sir."

Davidson put his cigar in the tray and came around the desk and grabbed Ederly's hand. "Good boy! I told old Barnhart you were our man!"

Ederly, in all the time he worked there, had never even seen Barnhart. All he knew was that Barnhart was an old man who had his living quarters on the sixth floor, and his private offices on the fifth floor.

The company brochure said that Barnhart had been a missionary on Banri Island before World War II, and was crucial in helping the British and American navies. After the war, he sent the King's two sons to Oxford to attend college. They returned to set up a government structure based on English law, form a national guard, and police force. Barnhart finally give up his ministry in exchange for a hundred year lease on certain parts of the island, and a similar contract to purchase native artifacts and craft wares at set prices. Evidently, the missionary was also a pretty good businessman.

Davidson put his arm around Ederly's shoulder and marched him to the door.

"Before you leave for the island, Robert, go pay a visit to Turner," Davidson said. "You might get something useful out of him…or maybe make sense of his gibberish."

"I'll do that, sir." Ederly said. Then, "Ah…about my pay, sir?" He knew, by reading the shipping documents he signed monthly, that all food and drink was shipped in to the remote enclaves, as well as the special jungle uniforms they wore. But he didn't know how they got paid.

"Your weekly pay will be at Island Headquarters in Port Runtang, with the finance officer. You can let it accumulate or get it once a week. However there isn't much you'll need it for on the island, though, unless you gamble and drink a lot."

"Oh well, alright then," the American said.

Actually he did like to drink and gamble. Perhaps going to the island wouldn't be such a bad thing after all, and if

9

things worked out smoothly he would soon be back in Hong Kong.

They stopped at the door for a moment. Ederly turned to face his boss. "They have a prison there, on the island, don't they, sir? I've heard they do."

"Yes, they do. It's just outside Port Runtang. Nasty place. That's why you have to keep your investigation on the hush."

"Because of the prison?" Ederly asked. "Why is that?"

"The police there are a crooked bunch. They'd just love to hang one on a *farangi*. They toss you into prison and you never get out. Their laws are part superstition and part fifteenth century. Never saw anything like it."

"A *'farangi'*, sir?"

"Yes, that's what they call us, *'farangi.'*"

Ederly shivered just thinking about the prison at Runtang. He suddenly regretted having given in so easily. But it was too late now. He was committed. There was no backing out.

Suddenly the phone on Davidson's desk started ringing.

10

"Hold on a moment, Robert."

Ederly stopped and waited. He wanted to leave.

Davidson went and picked up the phone. He stared at Ederly, one hand raised to get the young man's attention. He listened and spoke into the phone, too low for Ederly to hear. Finally he put the phone down.

"You don't have to go to the hospital, Robert," Davidson said with a sigh of resignation. "Turner went into a coma an hour ago…a severe case of botulism."

As he left, Ederly just shrugged and raised his eyebrows.

He never met Turner, and he really could care less about him.

2.

It was a typical tropical evening, hot and humid. Night birds were starting to call out in the deepening shadows. In the *bahn*, the two-story bamboo house with its tin roof, dinner was over. Little old Laa, the cook, had just cleared the table.

The people at the table were now left to peck at each other as they did every evening when the meal was over. Time and the jungle lay heavy on their hearts and minds, like a suffocating blanket.

Outside was the ever-present discordant clamor of insects and animals that signaled the setting of the sun. Those inside ignored the awful, piercing, primitive sounds. They had learned, over time, how to shut it all out. Drinking and talking worked best, so after dinner they usually spoke a lot of nonsense, just to hear each other's voices and to assure themselves they were still in touch with civilization.

"You ruined Turner, you know?" It wasn't a question, but an accusation that Ben Turner tossed at the young, sultry, seductive Ellen Goodstock.

"What?" Ellen was caught off guard for a moment, but quickly recovered. "Oh, the Yank? Phooey! I did no such thing."

Ben Smedley, a multi-chinned, huge mountain of flesh, decided to continue the assault. "Come now, my pretty. Admit it. You got him all gha-gha and googly. You made him your lackey-toady, is what you did, right Carver?"

"Oh, yes, Ellen, my sweet." The extremely tall and very skinny, hook-nosed Carver smelled blood. "We saw it all…what you did…how you did it."

"Poppycock!" Ellen shook head. Her curly, short, blond hair rippled about her neck. She blinked her purple hued eyes innocently, several times.

"Oh, you were very skillful, my dear." Smedley kept it going. His unruly brown hair hung down over his ears and forehead, almost covering his eyes.

Ellen defended herself vehemently with, "I certainly did not!"

But Carver was not so easily put off. "Oh, indeed you did, my love. Not to mention that revealing bathing suit that

13

you wore, but never got wet. You just laying around on the porch in it simply made the Yank's blood boil."

"Nonsense! You're all telling porkies on me," Ellen said. "I didn't do anything to that stupid man!"

They heard footsteps. Smedley looked to his right, at the doorway to the radio room.

"Oh, oh…here comes the Virgin Queen," he said with a chuckle.

"Say that to her face, Smedley, old chap, and she'd knock your block off," Ellen said.

In a few seconds Virginia Epley came from the radio room. She ignored those at the table and walked to the right, to the fully stocked bar by the outside wall. She got a glass, poured herself some scotch, took a drink, and shivered when it hit bottom.

"Virginia," Smedley called over, "any news from Port Runtang regarding Turner?"

"He turned critical. They evacuated him to the hospital in Hong Kong" Virginia Epley's voice was low register and manly. Like Ellen Goodstock, and the rest, she wore a man's short-sleeved khaki shirt tucked into a pair of jodhpurs,

14

tucked into a pair of riding boots. Suitable, rugged attire for this hotbed jungle oven called Banri Island.

Smedley smirked. "I hope the punk goes belly up! I really do. How about you, Carver?" Smedley's condescending voice was sometimes irritating.

"Me? To be truthful, Smedley, I don't care one way or another," Carver said, holding up his fingernails and staring at them as if they were more important than a man's life.

Miss Epley walked over and sat at the table alongside Carver, facing Ellen. She looked a bit miffed. She didn't like to be called by her first name. As the ramrod of the enclave, she preferred the formal, Miss Epley. If not Miss Epley, then just plain Epley. Smedley would pay for his mistake later, when he least expected it. Virginia Epley knew a thousand ways to make her subordinates feel miserable.

"They've already chosen someone to fill in during Turner's absence," Miss Epley said. "A man named, Ederly...Robert Ederly..." Then, "He'll be arriving in the next few days."

"That was rather quick, I'd say, wasn't it?" Ellen mused.

"Too damned quick, if you ask me," Smedley said. He shifted his weight in the rattan chair, making it squeal under his immense bulk.

Carver looked over the tips of his fingers and fluttered his eyelids. "Who is going to break him in?" Before anyone could answer, he said, "I'll do it, if you want me to?"

Smedley smirked sourly. "Sure you would, you fag! You would just love to, wouldn't you?"

The game was now on.

"Screw you, Smedley, old chap!"

Miss Epley cut in. "I was planning on letting Ellen have him."

Ellen stiffened in her chair. "Oh, no you don't. Not me. Let Carver have him."

"If I take him, what will you give me?" Carver asked.

"What do you want?"

"That red dress...the one with the spaghetti straps."

"What? The red one? Never!" Ellen said.

"Speaking of dresses, Ellen," Miss Epley said deciding she wanted to play, too. She winked at Smedley, "I wouldn't

16

mind getting into your blue, sequin topless, Ellen, with you in it, too, of course."

Carver and Smedley burst out into raucous laughter. Smedley's chair was on the verge of splintering under his weight. Ellen gave her boss a teasingly provocatively smile, but said nothing.

When things finally calmed down, Smedley took out a handkerchief and blew his nose and gasped for air. "My oh my! Tonight we are surrounded by dykes and fags, Ellen, my love! Perhaps we should join forces up in my room? Just you and I?"

Ellen smirked. "Of course, Smedley...right after you send out all those little native boys you have hidden there."

This sharp reply set Miss Epley and Carver to sputtering and giggling. Carver lost control and twisted in his chair and held his sides, jerking about like a puppet. His face turned purple.

"Good god, Carver," Smedley remarked. "Get a grip, old girl! You're falling apart!"

It was a few moments before control and silence set in as Carver's heavy breathing kept up for a while, then slowed down to normal.

"Did they go into detail about this new chap? Where he's from? What he looks like or anything like that?" Carver asked. He wiped tears off his cheeks with the back of his hand.

Miss Epley said, "No, not a thing."

"I hope he's not another bloody Yank!" Ellen said emphatically.

"Is somebody bringing him up or is coming alone?" Carver asked.

"I didn't ask," Miss Epley said.

"I mean, it's a long, scary drive. You don't want to break down on the road out there, all by yourself, even in the daytime, what with bandits and snakes all over the place." Carver sounded very fretful.

"Yes," Ellen said with mock concern. "Wouldn't that be just too awful?"

"I wonder what he looks like, did they say? No they wouldn't," Carver mused. "I wonder if he's young and handsome. That would be nice."

"You're such a bloody fag, Carver," Smedley smirked.

"Handsome or ugly," Miss Epley growled, "he pulls his weight around here, or he goes back to Hong Kong! After Turner, I've got no patience left for slackers and boozers!"

"Amen to that," Ellen said.

Carver got up and went over behind the bar. He reached under it and brought up a box of dominoes. The others got up, too, stretching.

"Anyone for dominoes?" Carver asked.

Miss Epley yelled over to Carver. "Maybe later…got some tidying up to do in the radio room before I put it to bed." She got up from the table with her glass of Scotch and went through the doorway to the radio room.

Ellen and Smedley went over to the bar and poured themselves a shot glass full of bourbon and sat down across from Carver. They watched as he dumped the dominoes out on the bar, turned them face down, and churned them around, mixing them. Finally they all drew nine tiles and set them on edge so they could read them.

"Ellen," Carver said, "they say we get much more rain on this side of the island than they do on the other side."

Ellen wasn't listening, but was concentrating on the tiles. "What? Oh, really?"

"Yes, and do you know why?"

Ellen, not interested, replied, "No…haven't the faintest idea."

"Well," Carver continued, "the currents are warmer on this side, you see? And that results in more moisture in the air, therefore…"

Smedley cut Carver off. "Carver! Carver! Who cares? It rains when it rains, and who gives a fig?"

Miffed, Carver shot back, "I was only trying to make conversation, Smedley. Small talk is all."

"Small talk is for small people, Carver," Smedley said. "So, put a cork in it, won't you, old chap?"

Carver suddenly glared at Smedley. "You bastard! You patronizing bastard! How dare you speak to me like that?"

He began to sob. "You can just go to hell, Smedley! Just go to hell!"

Carver tossed his drink in Smedley's face and rushed across the room to the stairs. He paused to look back a moment, then went up to his room, slamming the door. Moments later, Miss Epley appeared in the doorway, with drink in hand.

"What the blazes was that all about?" she asked.

Smedley got his handkerchief out and dabbed at his face. "Carver seems to be having a case of the vapors. It's that time of the month, I suppose." Then, "Awful waste of good liquor."

Ellen looked towards the stairs. She stood up, stretched, and yawned. "I'm bushed, folks. It's been a long day. Nighty-night, all."

As Ellen went up the stairs to her room, Miss Epley came over to sit at the bar facing Smedley. She topped off her drink and took a pull of scotch as the big man put the dominoes back in the box. He shoved the box over by the old, vintage Victrola at the end of the bar.

"Turner's replacement…this Ederly chap. I'm wondering about him Ben," Miss Epley said.

"Yes, so am I, Virginia," Smedley replied. He paused a moment: "How do you think we should play the bloke?"

"Cautiously…very cautiously."

"What if he starts asking questions about Turner?"

"If he does, then we'll know he's a Barnhart squealer, Ben."

"Well, if he tries anything slick with old Ben Smedley, he'll get more than he wants. I'll mangle the son of a bitch! I'll break his neck!"

Miss Epley chuckled. "Easy, Ben. A snake or scorpion in his bed would be neater."

"Yeah…that's a better idea."

There was a moment of silence. Suddenly the jungle sounds seemed louder and closer. They could hear some of the native workers talking in the yard. The smell of their bonfire floated in along with the sweet smell of *ghan cha*, the native form of marijuana.

"This Turner thing," Miss Epley said. "It puts the spotlight on us, and that's not good."

"Well, it's too late to change that now, isn't it?

"I wonder what old Barnhart is making of this?"

"He's probably pumping Turner for details so that he can lower the boom on us," Smedley mused.

"Yes, you're probably right."

"Well, whatever happens, Turner had best not show up here, again. Better for him if he croaked in that Hong Kong hospital. In my book, he's a dead duck...and I mean dead!

"I'll drink to that, Ben!" Miss Epley said.

They toasted to Turner's rapid demise.

"Did Ellen ever tell you what happened, what really happened, Ben?"

"No. You?"

"No. I tried to get it out of her, but she clams up whenever I mention Turner."

"It must have been pretty damn bad, seeing as how it threw her for a loop."

"Yeah...I sort of feel sorry for her. Turner was a real shit."

Smedley chuckled. "But, I think the fool was really in love with her."

"She'll never love anyone, Ben," Miss Epley said. "I think she's been hurt, in that field."

It started to rain. The drops hit hard on the tin roof above. Smedley refilled the glasses. There was a strange chill in the air.

3.

It was late Friday morning. Smedley and Carver were at the bar playing rummy. Ellen came downstairs and stopped to stretch and yawn before walking over to them.

"What time is it? Did I miss breakfast? Am I in trouble?" Ellen was groggy from oversleeping. She yawned again and sniffed.

"No, my dear," Smedley said, trying to concentrate on his cards, "and no going out on the road today because the supply truck is coming up from Runtang. Virginia wants us here to help unload it." He drew a card and laid one down.

"Yeah, I know, and I'm hungry," Ellen said.

"Go see Laa," Carver said. "She'll fix you up, my love." He drew a card and laid one down.

Ellen went off into the kitchen, next to the great room.

"Poor kid," Smedley said, "she's bored out of her skull."

"She should get out of here. She's got class. She could marry some rich guy and raise a family, instead of being stuck in this God forsaken place."

"Yeah? Well, what's keeping you here, old girl? Have you some skeletons to hide?"

"Oh, leave me alone…and knock off that, 'old girl' stuff, Smedley!" Carver said angrily.

"Tsk, tsk! Have the rag on, do we, my dear?"

"Screw you, you…you piece of blubber!"

"One step ahead of the law, are we, old chum? Are they looking for you back in jolly old London, are they?" Smedley kept it up.

"I might ask the same of you, Smedley. Didn't I see a wanted poster of you at jolly old Scotland Yard?"

Ellen came from the kitchen with tea and toast. She went to the dining table, sat down, and began to eat. She looked over at the bar, at Carver and Smedley.

"Where's Virginia?" Ellen asked.

"In the radio room," Smedley said, "trying to find out when the new chap is going to arrive."

"Maybe we'll get lucky and he'll meet up with some of those road bandits. I hear they patrol the Runtang road, sometimes," Ellen said.

"Heaven forbid!" Carver said. Then, "I just can't wait to meet this new fellow. He has such a romantic name. Robert Ederly... Roberto! Don't you just love it, Ellen?

"Carver, you're such a dildo...you really are!" Smedley chuckled.

Miss Epley came in from the radio room. She went to the bar.

Ellen called over. "What's the story on the new one, Epley? Anything?"

"He's coming up with Banks and Gilmore on the supply truck. They're going to take everything we have back today, when they leave."

Carver looked up from his cards. "He's on the supply truck? Well, that's pretty lousy!"

"I hope they put him in the back with the cartons of salted ham and sardines." Smedley said.

"I cancelled the sardines," Miss Epley said, glancing over at Ellen. "Nobody ate them anyway, except Turner."

"Why couldn't they have sent Ederly in style...in one of Barnhart's swanky cars?" Carver asked.

27

Ellen almost choked on her toast. "Who do you think he is, Carver? A big time movie star or something? You ninny! He's just a piss-ant, like the rest of us! My God!"

"One thing," Miss Epley said, seriously, "when he arrives, no more calling me 'Virginia.' It's, 'Miss Epley' or 'boss.' And no more palsy-walsy stuff with me in front of this guy. I had enough of that with that damn Yank Turner slapping me on the back and calling me 'Ginny.'"

They all looked a bit intense. Ederly wasn't even here yet but he had already made a change in their lives, and they didn't like it.

Smedley put down his cards. The game no longer interested him. "I'm guessing they broke down someplace on the road."

"I hope so," Ellen smirked. She went over to join the others at the bar.

"Maybe they forgot to fill up on petrol," Carver said. He tossed his cards down and scooped them all up and arranged them into a deck again. He put the deck back in the box. "They could have…"

"That would be nice," Smedley chortled. "That would be lovely!"

Miss Epley sneered, "Old Barnhart is too damn cheap to put radios in his vehicles. Someday that's going backfire on his Majesty!"

Smedley smiled. "I was just thinking…maybe they got hungry and stopped at one of those *bami* stands. They're all along the road." He chuckled. "Now, that's a pretty thought."

"Oh, dear," Carver said, "I do hope they warned him about that at headquarters. It's the first thing they told me not to do. Dysentery…brrrrrr…the runs…nasty stuff, that!"

"Yes," Miss Epley said, "that would be a crying shame, wouldn't it?" They all laughed hard.

Smedley finally calmed down enough to blurt out, "I remember the first time I ate at one of those *bami* stands. I got the poops for three weeks! I lost twenty pounds!"

That remark gave Carver a much awaited opening. "Oh, really? Then maybe you should eat there more often, old chap."

Smedley didn't appreciate the humor. "Don't get smart with me, you toothpick! I'll kick your bony arse, I will!"

Carver stopped smiling. "My goodness Smedley, I was just kidding. No need to get your knickers all in a wad. My gosh!"

There was a moment of calm. Finally, Miss Epley said, "Oh, I forgot to tell you, Runtang said that Turner kicked off."

"What? He went belly up?" Smedley asked. "You're kidding. Really?" He smiled. He was pleased.

"That's what they told me," Miss Epley said.

The room went quiet for a long time while they stole glances at each other.

"Did they say how he died?" Ellen finally asked.

"Food poisoning. They warned us to be careful…to inspect all canned food in the larder," Miss Epley said.

"It's this awful heat," Caver said. "You can hear the cans popping in the larder on a hot night. Poor, poor Turner, I'm going to miss playing dominoes with him. He loved playing dominoes."

"Poor Turner, my balls!" Smedley growled. "He was a skunk who died like a rat! That's all I have to say about Turner." He turned and looked over at Ellen. "Right, Ellen, my love?"

"I'd rather not talk about him, Smed, old chap," Ellen said. "If I never hear his name again, it'll be too soon. As far as I'm concerned, he never existed."

Smedley looked at Miss Epley. "Is Runtang or Hong Kong asking any questions about Turner?"

"So far, no," she said.

"Why should they ask any questions?" Ellen said. "Food poisoning is pretty common on the island, because of the intense heat and all."

"Quite so, Ellen, my dear," Smedley said. "A chap over at the east enclave came down with a pretty bad case only last month. Nobody questioned anybody about it...you get careless and it happens, that's all."

"Yes, but nobody died from it. That is, until now," Carver said.

"Well, maybe Turner had no resistance. He didn't eat properly and he drank all the time," Smedley said. "His

31

system couldn't cope with it, that's all. Look, none of us ever got sick, have we?"

Miss Epley said loudly, "Hey! Nobody is asking any questions about Turner, so don't get all spooked up about it." She inhaled and relaxed. "Hell, a month from now old Barnhart won't even remember his name. He probably doesn't even know we exist. He's too busy back there in his castle in Hong Kong, counting his money."

Smedley nodded in agreement. "Quite right, boss. Quite right."

Suddenly they all became alert as they heard the distant sound of a vehicle engine. It grew louder and louder by the second and finally, what sounded like a big truck, came through the enclave gate and stopped in front of the porch entrance. They all stayed in their places, waiting with sullen faces.

They knew it was the coming of Turner's replacement, but it felt more like the coming of an intruder. An intruder forcing his way into their world, a world closed to the outside, a special world they had constructed over a period of time, where they formed a set of rules of their own liking. He would never fit into their world. He'd have to be very special to do that. He would have to earn his way in, and that wasn't very likely to happen.

But even before he got close to them, they caught his scent. It was the scent of a different animal, and it made them wary and put them on their guard. They knew that they had to be fearful of this intruder because he would try to bring their world crashing down around their ears. They would have to be on their toes at all times.

Suddenly they heard his footsteps as he slowly walked up the stairs onto the screened-in porch that ran around the front of the house. He came in through the open doorway there, near the bar, and stood with a big grin on his face, looking them over.

They all stared back at him, a tall, handsome, young man, dressed in soiled, wrinkled tropical whites, especially filthy at the knees. He carried a well-worn army duffle bag. The words stenciled across it were no longer readable. He dropped the bag inside the doorway, smiled, and nodded.

"Hi, folks! I'm Robert Ederly! Sorry I'm late. We had a flat tire and ran into a ditch a ways back. We had trouble getting the wheel off." A pause as he looked around, as if he thought he was something special. "Well, folks, here I am!"

In the background they heard the truck moving further down the yard.

"Oh, cripes," Ellen muttered under her breath, "just another damn, nutty Yank!" Ederly glanced at her, almost as if he had heard her words. He smiled.

"Where's Banks and Gilmore?" Miss Epley asked sharply.

"They're taking the truck down to the shed area, to get the flat fixed. They said to meet them at the larder," Ederly reported.

Miss Epley stared at the intruder for a moment, then got up from the bar and walked towards the kitchen door.

"Alright, people, let's go into the larder, and unload the shit-paper and food. They'll be wanting to get back on the road as soon as possible." She added, "You too, Yank!"

They all followed Miss Epley into the kitchen. Laa, the cook, stood aside and quietly watched as they opened the door to the larder, and went past the rows of food and supplies to the back door, to where Banks had backed the truck up. The larder was actually a shed-like extension build onto the outer wall of the kitchen. Its rear door opened into the yard.

Banks and Gilmore climbed into the back of the truck and handed out all the items that Miss Epley had ordered from Runtang. Smedley, Carver, and Ellen, worked while Ederly stood wide-eyed, looking around.

"Hop to it, Yank!" Miss Epley growled at him.

"Oh, sorry, ma'am," Ederly said and got in line behind Ellen.

The unloading took less than an hour. When all the cooking oil, lye soap, sugar, salt, pepper, tea, flour, canned fruits, canned meats, and toilet paper were unloaded, and the cylinders of natural gas for Laa's stove were locked in a separate wire cage, Banks moved the truck further down the yard to the big shed where the native wares were stored. This task took longer and in about three hours the truck was full and the bins were empty. By then the flat tire was fixed and put in its rack on the truck.

"Nice load," Banks said to Miss Epley. "Runtang will be happy." Gilmore nodded his approval.

Miss Epley smiled. "Tell Runtang to kiss my ass, Banks, old chap!"

Banks chuckled. "Sure I will, Miss Epley. I always do." Everybody laughed, except Ederly, who seemed to be a bit confused. He already felt like an outsider.

"Come in for a drink before you go," Miss Epley offered. They all went back into the house.

4.

Banks and Gilmore stayed an hour and then started back to Runtang. Ederly settled in. He was assigned a room up on the second floor next to Carver's. He showered, shaved, and put on a clean set of tropical whites.

When he came down for dinner, he stood out like a sore thumb against the others who wore their khaki short-sleeved shirts, jodhpurs, and riding boots. He did have the correct uniform, but had hung it in the closet. After all, the day was shot, so he saw no reason to wear it until tomorrow.

They finished eating and sat there at the table relaxing.

"That was a delicious meal," Ederly said.

"Yes," Miss Epley remarked. "Laa works miracles."

"The fish was great. What was it?"

"A native fish, called *kham-pet*. From the lake," Carver said. "It's always good with rice, broccoli raab, and mango sauce."

"It was fantastic. I'll have to ask her for her recipe," Ederly said, just to make conversation.

37

"Do you cook?" Smedley asked unexpectedly.

"Well, no," Ederly replied, caught off guard.

"Then you don't really need the recipe, do you, old chap?"

"Well…ah…I guess I don't, then."

"No, you don't, then."

Carver broke in to cut the tension. "Ederly, where are you from?"

Ederly paused, and then said, "The east coast…Rhode Island."

"So, what brought you all the way over here, Ederly?" Miss Epley asked.

"Ah...what brought me here?"

"Yes? What?"

"Work, I guess."

Smedley chuckled. "He guesses. He's not sure. He doesn't know."

"Well, it's sort of a long story, really," Ederly said. "And pretty dull, too."

"Oh, do tell us, Ederly," Carver said. "I just love stories. We're so isolated out here, you know."

Ellen smirked. "Yes, Ederly, we just love stories. Don't we, Smed, old boy?"

"Oh, indeed we do!" Smedley rolled his eyes, pretending to be interested.

Ederly looked a bit uncomfortable. "Ah, well, as I said I'm from Rhode Island. After college, I volunteered for the Korean War..."

Smedley cut in, "What Division were you with, in Korea?"

"Division?"

"Yes. You know what a Division is, don't you, old boy?"

Ederly laughed nervously. "Is this a test? Why all the questions?"

Miss Epley explained, "Well, you're new here, Ederly, so we're just curious about you, that's all. There's nothing wrong with that, is there?"

"No, I guess not," Ederly said. Then, "Yes, well I was with a Regiment, if that's what you mean?"

"But you were under a Division too, right?" Smedley persisted.

"Ah…sure. The Seventh Division." Ederly didn't sound too sure.

Ederly suddenly felt trapped. He didn't want to come right out and say, "Well, guys, I spent my tour in Korea back in Seoul, behind a desk with an Intelligence Battalion, and going out to parties every night at the Officer's Club!" So, he said the first thing that popped into his head, the Seventh Division, a unit he had heard of.

"Armor? Artillery? Infantry? Engineer?" Smedley asked. Ederly wished the man would just shut his fat mouth.

Ederly picked one, "Ah…Engineer."

Miss Epley said, "You never really answered my question, Ederly."

"Which question was that, ma'am?"

"About how you came on board?"

"On board? I don't understand. Oh, with Barnhart, you mean?"

"Yes, in Hong Kong, with Barnhart?"

"Do you know Mr. Davidson?" Ederly asked.

"Sure," Miss Epley said. "He works back in Hong Kong, in the Barnhart Building, in shipping. He's an idiot."

"Yes…ah…well, I met him when I was in Hong Kong for two weeks rest, during the Korean War." Ederly told the story how he met Davidson, and so forth.

"Did you go out to the racetrack while you were in Hong Kong?" Ellen asked.

"Oh, yes, the race track. Everybody goes there."

"Sure," Smedley said, "everybody goes out to the…what's it called…ah, do you remember what it's called, Ellen?"

"Uh…no, not right off hand, but Ederly knows. What's it called, Ederly?"

Ederly suddenly felt as if he was being ganged up on. He had been to the racetrack but for some reason he just couldn't remember the damn name. He felt a bit disoriented.

41

"Ah, the racetrack? Yes, ah, it was right on the tip of my tongue. Sorry, I just can't think of it right now. Isn't that stupid of me?"

There was a moment of silence. They all stared at Ederly. His face was flushed and he felt as if he was a bug under a magnifying glass. Finally Miss Epley said, "Smedley, have you checked Ederly's room for visitors?"

Ederly suddenly came alert. "Visitors?"

"Yes. We get them all the time. They sort of hide away, so you won't notice them. There's this jade green scorpion and this tiny red and black snake…all very lethal. Also, there's that little spider, the Brown Recluse, I think it's called. It loves to sleep in your shoes, overnight."

"You're kidding me, right?" Ederly said.

"Believe me, I'm not!" Miss Epley said. "Carver, take Ederly up to his room and show him how to check for visitors, won't you, please?"

Carver got up. "Come on, Ederly, I'll show you the ropes." Ederly got up and followed Carver upstairs to his room. Miss Epley, Ellen, and Smedley sat smiling as they watched them go.

Smedley snickered. "I think you just scared the crap out of the Yank, Virginia."

"What do you think of him, Smedley?" Miss Epley asked.

"What do I think? I think he's a Barnhart spy," Smedley growled through clenched teeth. "That's what I think. A stinking spy. A fink and a squealer."

"Are you sure?"

"All I know is there's something not quite right about this bloke," Smedley said.

"He never once mentioned Turner, or asked about him," Ellen said, "and he was in Hong Kong when Turner showed up in the hospital."

"Yeah," Smedley said, His eyes narrowed. "Good point, Ellen, my dear. After all, the Yank is Turner's replacement, so you'd expect him to ask about what happened to him, wouldn't you?"

"That's my point," Ellen said. "He's acting as if he never even heard of Turner."

Miss Epley sighed. "Well, what should we do about it? What's the best course to take?"

"Maybe I should just beat the truth out of him," Smedley said. "Just kick his arse until he talks."

Epley held that vision in her mind for a second. She smiled. "No, at least not yet. But keep that thought, Smedley. We might just have to do that. But right now I've got a better idea."

"Oh?" Smedley said. "What's that?"

"Compromise him. Compromise him good. Turn his head. Get him dirty…as dirty as the rest of us."

Miss Epley chuckled and looked at Ellen. "Maybe you didn't notice the way he looks at our girl, here. From the first moment he came through the door, all he could see was her."

"I guess I missed that," Smedley said.

"That's because you're a man, Smedley," Miss Epley said. "Yes…I think the Yank has a sweet tooth, and all we have to do is give him some candy to chew on."

"Oh, no!" Ellen said. "I see where this is going, and I won't do it! Keep that damn Yank away from me or he'll end up just like…" She suddenly realized what she was about to say and stopped. "I'll quit, first!"

Miss Epley turned towards Ellen, and stared at her for a moment. "Listen, this is not just about Turner. It's about everything, this whole place. If this bloke gets nosey, he might get lucky, and it will all come out, and quitting won't be an option."

"What do you mean, quitting won't be an option?"

Smedley cut in. "She means it's Runtang Prison for all of us, if everything comes out. And you don't want to end up in Runtang Prison. It's a dark, damp, nasty hole you'll never get of…never. You get one meal a day, fish heads, and rice with worms in it. Think about that, my dear."

Ellen sighed in resignation. "Okay, okay! What do you want me to do, jump his bones?

"No," Miss Epley said. "Just be friendly…and available…"

"Available? What the heck does that mean?"

"Best be careful, though," Smedley said. "You don't want to gush all over him. He'll get suspicious."

They heard footsteps above and Carver came down the stairs into the great room and stood by the table.

"Well?" Miss Epley asked. "Where's the Yank?"

"He's taking a nap. He said he'd been partying all night in Port Runtang. He's exhausted."

"Oh, my," Smedley said. "Our boy likes to party. Did you get that, Ellen, old girl? You two should get on famously, don't you think?"

"Sure," Ellen said sarcastically. "No one likes to party more than I do." She paused. "Crap! What did I do to deserve two Yanks in a row?"

"He's been shot," Carver said seriously.

"Who's been shot?" Miss Epley asked.

"The Yank," Carver answered. "I saw the scar on his side. The bullet went in and out. He got a medal, a Silver Star for Valor. After that he got transferred to the rear, to a desk job."

No one spoke for a while. Finally Smedley said, "Hell, anyone can buy a medal, right, Ellen?" Ellen only shrugged and looked away.

"I also saw the citation letter," Carver said. "It had his name on it. You think that's a fake, too, Smedley, you son of a bitch?"

Carver turned and took his skinny body over to the bar and poured himself a drink. "Anyone for dominoes?" They all ignored him. He said in a low voice, just loud enough for them to hear, "You bunch of hypocrites!"

"Christ," Smedley chuckled, "Carver is already in love with the Yank."

"The way you people treated him, it was disgusting," Carver said, his voice cracking. He looked about to cry.

Ellen went over and put an arm around Carver.

"Better buck up, old stump," she said. "This isn't going to be tiddly-winks. It's going to get messy, and you're either with us or against us, Carver."

Carver sighed and nodded.

5.

The following day, was a Saturday. Everyone was left to do whatever they felt inclined to do. By evening Ellen, Carver, and Smedley were gathered at the bar talking and drinking. Ederly stayed in his room all that time.

"He's been in his room since last evening," Smedley remarked. Maybe he died in his sleep."

"I don't think so," Carver said. "I heard him snoring when I came past his room a while ago."

"He should be hungry when he wakes up," Ellen said. "He hasn't eaten since last night, at dinner."

Smedley nodded. "Go up there and wake him, Carver. He needs to eat or he'll be too weak to work. And we don't want that."

"Alright," Carver said.

He got up from the bar and went up the stairs to Ederly's room. In a few minutes he and Ederly came down the stairs. Ederly stopped to stretch and yawn. His tropical whites were wrinkled, as if slept in. He and Carver went over to the bar.

"Welcome back to life," Smedley said in a friendly voice.

Ederly sat at the bar and chuckled. "Yeah, I guess I did sleep the sleep of the dead, didn't I?"

"Hey, so what? It's Saturday, and we're off the clock until Monday," Smedley went on. "So, enjoy it while you can, my friend."

Ellen went into the kitchen while the men made small talk. A few minutes later she came out with a tray of crackers, jam, and cold tea. She set it on the dining table and called to Ederly. He got up from the bar and went over to sit across from her.

"Where's Miss Epley?" he asked.

"In the radio room."

"Does she call Runtang often?"

"At least three times a day." Ellen said as Ederly slathered jam on a cracker and started eating. "Morning, noon, and night." Ederly stared at her and chuckled. "What's so funny about that?" she asked.

"Nothing… I was wondering why you're being so nice to me all of a sudden," Ederly said. "You hardly noticed me before."

"Would you feel better if I called you a dumb-assed Yank?" she asked.

"Ah… no!"

Miss Epley came from the radio room and stopped at the table. She looked down at Ellen and Ederly.

"Get enough rest, Ederly?"

"Yes ma'am, I sure did."

"Good," Miss Epley said as she walked over to the bar. She got a full bottle of whiskey, and went out onto the screened-in porch, and then into the yard. Carver and Smedley followed her.

"Where are they going?" Ederly asked.

"Down to the village."

"What's down there? A party?"

"It's all about public relations. We have to be nice to the *Phu-yai*…the village chief."

"Oh, yeah. Diplomacy."

"Exactly. Winning them over and all that, otherwise we don't get any native wares or artifacts," Ellen explained. "It's like that all over the island. You have to get them on your side." Then, "Don't move, Ederly. I'll be right back."

Ellen got up and went into the kitchen. Moments later she returned with a small bowl of little, elongated, dark green pepper things. She sat down next to Ederly and put the bowl in front of him. He suddenly became aware of the scent of her flesh and hair, everything. He stared at her.

"You're staring, Ederly," Ellen said softly. "Don't stare."

"You're very beautiful," Ederly said.

Ellen ignored his remark and picked up a pepper. She held it up, inches from his mouth.

"What's this?"

"Doctor's orders, open wide."

Ederly opened his mouth and Ellen shoved the raw pepper in. "Chew!" she ordered. Without hesitating, he began to chew rapidly. Seconds later his mouth felt as if it was full of fire ants. His eyes watered and blurred. "That's a good boy," he heard her say. "Finish it off! The next one won't hurt a bit. You'll see."

Suddenly she had somehow managed to pop two more peppers into his mouth. He chewed rapidly and swallowed.

Just when he couldn't stand anymore, she shoved a cracker with jam on it between his lips. He chewed that, too. It tasted sweet and it quickly eased the pain, He asked for another cracker and she gave it to him. Finally she had him gulp down a cold cup of sugary tea. Then it was all over.

"Good-boy," Ellen said.

"What was that all about?" he asked.

"Parasites," Ellen said.

"Parasites? What parasites?"

"In the stomach. Didn't they mention it back in Runtang?"

"I guess I wasn't paying attention."

"Well, that's just one of the many side benefits of working for Barnhart."

"So, you eat those little, green devils to prevent stomach parasites, do you?"

"Uh...huh! Once a month. Miss Epley's orders. That's what the natives do, too."

Ellen turned her face to Ederly. Their eyes connected. "What did he say about me?" she asked.

"Who?" He was staring at her mouth as if he wanted to kiss it.

"Turner...what did he tell you?"

"Nothing."

"You're lying. I can see it in your face. Come on, it's just between you and me, okay?"

"I never spoke to Turner," Ederly said. "He went into a coma before I could ever visit him in the hospital."

"Okay, if you say so." It was obvious she didn't believe him.

Ellen got up and went to the bar. Ederly followed. She stood behind the bar and took out two glasses. She filled them with bourbon. He stood facing her.

"Let's toast," Ellen said.

"Alright...to what?"

"To Barnhart…may the old fart live forever! Otherwise we'll all be out of a job."

They laughed and drank. Ellen topped off their glasses.

"Let's toast to Miss Epley. She a real bitch!" They toasted again and Ellen topped of their glasses again.

"I think you're trying to get me drunk," Ederly said.

"Now, why would I do that?"

"I don't know…maybe you're trying to take advantage of me?"

"Sure, you're irresistible, Ederly."

"I know."

"Bottoms up, Yank," Ellen said.

They both took another drink. Ellen put her glass down and walked over to the open doorway that led to the screened-in porch. When Ederly came up behind her, she stepped out onto the porch and walked up close to the screen and inhaled the cool, musty, jungle air. They stood in the shadows, looking into the deserted yard.

With everyone gone it was quiet, even in the kitchen. Laa had returned to her family in the village. The workers were gone too, so the yard was empty and silent. There was a bit of moon out so they could see the black outline of the jungle canopy outside the high enclave fence.

Unseen insects and night creatures spoke to one another, some loud, some soft. Ellen and Ederly listened for a while.

"How far to the village?" Ederly asked.

"Not far," Ellen said. "It's by the lake. You can't see it from here."

"Where did you come from?" Ederly asked.

"Jolly old London."

"That's nice."

"Not really. Where I came from it was filthy and smelly."

"Were you ever in love… in London?"

"In London, very body falls in love at least once. It's the law." Ellen said. "Mine ended badly, so I'd rather forget about London. And you? Ever in love?"

"Not so far. I hear it hurts."

Ellen chuckled. "Oh, it can hurt. But it can be nice, if you find the right person."

Ederly was studying her face in the moonlight, the way it played off her contours. Her eyes seemed to reflect little diamonds.

"You're staring again, Ederly," Ellen said softly. "Please don't."

"Sorry…" He looked out into the darkness.

"You know what I like about this place?" Ellen said.

"No, tell me."

"It's frozen in time. It stays the same and no one knows we're here. We're invisible to the outside world," Ellen said.

"Except for Barnhart. He knows where we are."

"But that's the thing…he's stuck in the past too, just like we are. It's all his doing, you know."

"Well, it's still 1959 in Hong Kong…and here, too," Ederly said.

"I don't care about Hong Kong. I'm comfortable and safe right here in my own private little world," Ellen said. She turned to look at Ederly. "Carver said you were wounded in Korea. Show me where."

Ederly took her hand and placed it on his side, above his belt. "Here…"

"I can feel the bump. It's warm, does it hurt?"

"No, but it itches when it rains," Ederly said. He put his own hand over her hand. He bent to kiss her but she turned her head and pulled away.

She walked back to the bar and he followed her. She went to the old Victrola at the end of the bar, put on a record, and cranked it up. It started playing and a hollow, high pitched male voice began singing, "…meet me tonight in dreamland…under a silvery moon…"

They each took a drink of whiskey and listened. Ellen said, "Do you dance, Ederly?"

"A little."

Ellen led Ederly over into the empty shadows in the spot between the bar and the great room. She fitted nicely into his arms. They didn't move much, just held on to each other and swayed back and forth and around in small circles. His heart was pounding, and he felt the whiskey begin to take hold.

"You're a bad dancer," Ellen said.

"I'm a bit drunk."

"You can't hold your whiskey, can you?"

"No, I'm more of a beer person."

"Sure you are…sure you are," She whispered softly with her lips against his ear.

They just clung together. He held her tight. They didn't move. Suddenly he felt something warm and wet on his shirt. She started to shake. She was crying softly. Suddenly she pushed him away and turned and walked over to the stairs.

"What's wrong?" he asked. "Did I do something?"

"I'm sorry, Ederly," she said. "I'm very tired and I have a headache. Good-night."

He watched her as she went up to her room. Soon he heard her lock the door. Ederly went behind the bar and refilled his glass and sat there listening to the music. When it was finished, he rewound the Victrola and played it again. He wondered when Miss Epley, Carver, and Smedley would come back.

Finally he went up to his room.

6.

It was Monday morning, time to get serious and go back to work. Miss Epley, Ellen, Smedley, and Carver were gathered around the dining table in the great room, where Epley had laid out a map. She held a pointer in one hand. Next to the map were two sacks of coins, and two PRC-6, battery operated, army surplus radios.

"Carver! Go get the Yank! Drag his ass down here naked, if you have to!"

Suddenly Ederly, dressed in a short sleeved khaki shirt, jodhpurs, and riding boots, came rushing out of his room and down the stairs and over to the table. For some reason, the clothes made him look a bit silly, as if he was auditioning for a grade-B jungle movie.

"Sorry," he murmured. Epley gave him a withering look. He almost cringed. She took a second look at how he looked in his uniform and stifled a giggle.

"Ellen," Epley began, "you and Ederly will go to *Bahn-du-Mah*. Smedley, you and Carver will go to *Bahn-du-Nam*. Any questions?"

"I don't need anybody," Ellen said. "I can handle it alone."

"No, nobody leaves this enclave alone," Miss Epley said. "It's the rule."

"Then, why doesn't Ederly go with Carver, and Smedley go with me?"

"Because I said he'd go with you, that's why, and that's that! Get it?"

Ellen pouted. "Yeah, I get it."

"Very good, then," Miss Epley said. She stared around at them for a moment. "Last month we just barely made our quota. We're going to have to fill the bins again. If we don't, Runtang is going to think were screwing off. So, I'm expecting everyone to come back here with a full load."

Smedley sighed. "I say screw Runtang! If they think it's so easy, let them come up here and try it! We're doing our best!"

"I know, and I appreciate it," Epley said. "But the pressure is on, and I can't do anything about it."

"I could have bought more the last time," Smedley said, "but I ran short of *raht*."

"Well, I put five-hundred more coins in each bag. That should be more than enough, this time."

Ederly coughed for attention. "What's a *raht*?"

"It's coin of the realm, Ederly," Miss Epley said. "Something that Barnhart and the King's sons came up with."

"What's it worth?"

"In dollars and pounds? Nothing. You can buy a barrelful for a British pound. But we still have to account for every bit of it to Runtang. They want an accounting for everything, from toilette paper to pencils, the bastards!" Miss Epley let that sink in for a moment, and then said. "Any more questions? No? Good. Just remember, get back here before dark. I repeat... get back in here before dark!"

They all nodded. Ellen and Smedley picked up the sacks of money and the radios, and went out into the yard, with Ederly and Carver close on their heels. They went across the hard-packed dirt yard to a large shed where two U.S. Army surplus two and a half ton cargo trucks sat waiting.

Native mechanics, dressed in khaki trousers and sandals, stood next to each truck. They held wrenches and dirty rags in their hands. They nodded to the Barnhart people and stepped aside to let them get into the trucks. Ellen got behind the wheel, while Ederly sat in the passenger's seat. She stowed the radio in the glove compartment and put the money sack on the seat between her and Ederly. He noticed a snakebite kit in the compartment.

"Snakes?" Ederly asked.

"Yes, lots of snakes, Ederly." She turned on the ignition switch and hit the starter pedal. The engine coughed, backfired twice, and then died. Ellen tried again and finally got it started. She saw the uncertain look on Ederly's face and chuckled.

"Relax, Yank."

"You want me to drive? I drove one of these old babies in Korea."

"Nobody drives my truck," Ellen said. "Nobody but me. Got that?"

"Yes, ma'am," Ederly said with a shrug.

Moments later they were going through the enclave gate out, onto a dirt road, and heading northwest. The sun was out in a cloudless, deep blue sky, and the view ahead was clear.

The road was narrow and sometimes they had to veer to the right to let carts, pulled by water buffalos, pass by. They drove past small villages and forded streams. Once the road ran through a long stretch of nothing but jungle where dark green overgrowth formed a tunnel over the road. Ellen had to put on the headlights to avoid running into a canal-like ditch. Ederly noticed how well she handled the big, six geared truck.

"So, what do the natives do with all this funny money," Ederly asked.

"They spend it."

"Where? I haven't noticed any Sears and Roebucks anywhere around here."

"They go to Runtang. Everything is there…stores, movies, bars. There's even a mission church to convert the natives, and a native run radio station."

"Oh, that's nice."

"Sure it is," Ellen sneered. "Nice for Barnhart. He owns it all, even the bank."

Ederly chuckled. "Why am I not surprised?" Then, "That's a pretty good deal. He makes the money, buys their artifacts with it, and then gets the money back when they spend it at places and on stuff he owns."

"Sure, but they get something out of it, too," Ellen said. "Everything they buy is a luxury to them. Generators, radios, electric appliances, stuff that makes their lives easier."

"Sounds like you're defending him."

"He was a missionary here years ago. He's done a lot of good. The old man has created a thriving economy here, where there used to be a primitive barter system. There's nothing wrong with that, is there?"

"No, I guess not," Ederly said. "I guess not."

It started to get hot in the cab of the truck, so they rolled down the windows on both sides to let air in. When that didn't help, they cranked open the windshield a few inches. That caused the canvas top above them to whip in the wind, making a snapping sound, but the breeze felt good.

Three hours later they came into the village of *Ban-du-Mah.*

A narrow road led straight in past small thatched huts to a large, open area. Ellen drove in a half circle, stopped, and backed the truck up under a large shed-like structure where some natives were milling around. Ederly grabbed the money sack and they got out and walked over to meet the *Phu-yai,* the village chief.

Ellen performed the ceremonial *wai,* bowing her head and putting her palms flat together in front of her chin, with fingers extended, saying, *"Sah-wah-dee."* It was the equivalent of shaking hands and saying, "Hello, how are you?"

A generator purred in the background.

"This is *Khune* Ederly," Ellen said as she took the money sack from Ederly. Ederly was about to shake hands but reconsidered and did a *wai,* as best as he could.

"Ederly," Ellen said. "Go back to the truck and take a look at the operation. You'll learn something."

Ellen and the *Phu-yai* went into a hut larger than the rest. A generator hummed nearby, and Ederly could hear a voice that obviously came from a radio. It was in the Banri language. To him it sounded like a religious sermon or an advertisement for a product. He listened a moment and went back to the truck.

He stood and watched as several natives, both men and women, got woven baskets filled with handmade craft wares and native artifacts from under the shed. They put them into the bed of the truck, using straw as a buffer between them. There were hand woven rugs, placemats, hats, and fans made from palm fronds, all dyed in bright colors.

There were also small, strange looking figurines and musical instruments such as flutes, carved from hardwood. Ederly noticed larger figures molded from fired clay, and a large selection of pottery in the form of kiln-baked cups and bowls and plates, all in dazzling colors.

Much of it looked like crude, cheaply made eye candy, but it had a certain innocence about it. It was made by individual hands and had a sincerity of effort, of pride and of authenticity.

It took over an hour to fill the truck. When they were finished, the natives turned their attention to Ederly, and crowded around him, talking in their own language, but tossing in a few English words, too. The young girls, especially, took an interest in him, and he caught the words...movie star...good looking. They had no inhibitions about touching him. When it got too intense, he quickly got into the cab of the truck. They finally left laughing.

A few moments later Ellen came and got in beside him. As they drove away she held up the money sack and smiled.

"Got some left. Epley will be happy," she said.

"How does it work? Who sets the price?"

"Nobody."

"That's crazy! I never heard of such a thing."

"Well, you did now."

"Suppose you don't agree to his price?"

"It's like following a script in a play. We all know our lines. If I tell him I have four-hundred *raht*, he knows that I really have five-hundred, so he'll ask for four-hundred and fifty. That way, no one is embarrassed. He gets what he wants and Barnhart gets what he wants."

"And that's it? That's what it's all about? Not offending Barnhart?"

"That's pretty much it. Basically, the chief doesn't want to offend the old fart."

"Oh…I see." Actually, it didn't make any sense to Ederly.

They drove on. By then it was midafternoon and the sun was low in the west. A few miles on and Ederly began to notice how the truck didn't bounce around so much because of the load in back. They had to stop and wait once as a farmer marched his pigs and ducks across the road.

"If you ever hit one," Ellen said, "you'll have to pay for it out of your own pocket, or go to prison."

"Oh, really?"

"Yes, really."

"You ever hit one?"

"Not yet, but I came close, once."

Ederly chuckled. This had been a fun day.

Two hours later they drove in through the enclave gate and over to the storage sheds. Smedley and Carver were already there, unloading, when Ellen backed in. Two natives came over and lowered the tailgate. One climbed up in back and began to hand stuff down to the other one who put it on a shelf inside the shed with other items of the same kind.

"Don't you keep track?" Ederly asked.

"Not now. We do that when we send a shipment down to the warehouse in Runtang," she said.

"Runtang runs a pretty loose operation."

Ellen chuckled. "It's tighter than it looks."

They left the truck and went over to the house, into the great room. Smedley and Ellen put the money sacks and the radios on the table. Miss Epley picked up the money sacks and shook them. She nodded.

"Nice work," she said. "Too bad I have to tell you this, but...guess what?"

"Oh, no!" Carver said.

"Shite!" Smedley growled.

"What's wrong?" Ederly asked.

"They've scheduled us for an inventory...this very Friday, the bastards!" Miss Epley growled.

7.

It was late Friday morning, and the sky was overcast, when Banks and Gilmore, the two company men, drove up from Port Runtang in a silver Pierce Arrow. They were both wearing side arms. They quickly got out of the front seat, and opened the rear doors for Mr. Marsden.

Mr. Marsden was a short, pudgy, roly-poly man in his fifties. His stomach bulged slightly. He was bald on top, but had tuffs of black hair on the sides. He was dressed in a tailor made, expensive, light gray, silk suit. With him was an accountant and an accountant's assistant.

They carried briefcases while Mr. Marsden carried a superior look on his pasty, pale face.

As soon as they had heard the car coming, Miss Epley assembled her crew out in the yard to greet the official visitors. In fact, Virginia Epley stood at mock attention while the others stood behind her in a neat row. All of them, including her, had clean uniforms, if short sleeved khaki shirts, jodhpurs, and riding boots, could be considered as a uniform.

"Mr. Marsden, sir!" Miss Epley said, extending her right hand. Mr. Marsden barely touched it, and greeted her with a, "harrumph!" He followed that with a blank stare, but his face lightened up as soon as he saw Ellen Goodstock. His eyes did a sort of roguish dance, and he cracked a slight smile.

It suddenly began to rain and Mr. Marsden made an abrupt turn and hurried towards the house with the accountants close on his heels. Miss Epley and the others stood staring after him for a moment.

"How come the pistols?" Miss Epley asked Gilmore as they walked slowly towards the porch.

"His idea," Gilmore said. "He's afraid we'll get kidnapped by bandits." They all chuckled.

"I never shot one of these in my life," Banks said.

It started to rain harder so they ran. They went across the yard, up on the porch, and into the house. Inside, they stood before Mr. Marsden in the great room, by the dining table, and felt the overwhelming aura of his self-importance. He had a superior smile on his small, pudgy mouth as he took their measure with his dead, pale green, dull eyes. Those eyes eagerly fell on Ellen, and she gave him a big, happy smile, which he quickly returned. She, and Miss

Epley, knew right then and there that they now had the leverage they so badly needed.

"Why don't you introduce me to your staff, Miss Epley," Mr. Marsden said, a little less formally.

Miss Epley went through the motions, saving Ellen for last. "And, sir, last, but not least, Miss Ellen Goodstock."

Mr. Marsden stared hungrily at the eye candy before him. For the moment everyone else was forgotten. "Don't tell me you actually drive one of those big bad trucks now, do you, Miss Goodstock?"

"I do, sir," Ellen replied in a giggly-girly sort of way.

"And you actually go out into the field?"

"Yes, sir."

"Aren't you afraid of all those awful snakes, and terrible bandits?"

"No, sir," Ellen cooed. Ederly noticed that she was several inches taller than Mr. Marsden. He stifled a chuckle.

"Very commendable, young lady! Very commendable!" Then, "Ah…by any chance, do you dance?"

"Sir?" Ellen asked, innocently.

72

"Do you enjoy dancing, Miss Goodstock?"

"Yes, I do sir," she purred, letting her eyes flutter.

"Do you tango, by any chance?"

"Not very well, I'm afraid." Ellen kept playing the ingénue.

Mr. Marsden nodded and continued to stare at Ellen, as if hypnotized. Suddenly, he shook the spell off and quickly got down to business.

"Shall we begin?" The accountants had already taken over the dining table in the great room, and spread out all the preprinted inventory sheets. "This shouldn't take long."

"Would you like something to eat first, sir?" Miss Epley asked.

"Sandwiches and tea, while we work, would be fine," Mr. Marsden said, as if speaking to a waitress.

Miss Epley nodded at Ellen. "Miss Goodstock, would you go help Laa with sandwiches and tea?"

"Yes, ma'am," Ellen said and went into the kitchen. Mr. Marsden's eyes watched her go.

The inventory then officially began.

Once a year, Miss Epley, had to sign again for all company property at the enclave. There was a pre-typed, itemized set of inventory sheets with headings and subheadings that listed all the things in the house, or *bahn*, as the natives called it. All tangible items such as the kitchen stove, and cookware, and all silverware and dinnerware, were to be counted. The chairs and tables were also included, but not the expendables, such as the food and toilet paper.

Also there was the equipment in the radio room and the radio antennae on the roof. In the yard there were the two large trucks, two small trucks, and two jeeps, and the five mechanic's tool sets used by the natives to repair the trucks and the 5KW generator that supplied the electricity.

Then there was the water pump and the portable water purification system, excluding the chemicals, which fell under consumables. At the bottom of the list were the smaller items such as locks and keys, a typewriter, and several garbage cans, and so forth. Each item had to be seen and examined and checked off the list, which meant a lot of footwork and time.

Before the work began, Mr. Marsden took his men aside and had a short talk out of earshot of the rest. After that, when they started on the inventory, Miss Epley noticed that they worked very slow and were very talkative. They asked a lot of irrelevant questions, like, "Nicely kept frying pan...how long have you had this one?" or "I used to have an old typewriter like this. They don't make them any better nowadays." They dawdled along like snails while, at every chance he got, the suave Mr. Marsden cornered Ellen Goodstock in idle chitchat. The rest stood by, watching from the sidelines.

"This shouldn't take long, should it?" Ederly asked

"It's a one day job at best," Miss Epley said. "But don't expect them to leave before Monday."

"He's going to stretch it out that long? Why?" Ederly asked.

"Lots of reasons," Miss Epley said.

"For instance?" Ederly persisted.

"For instance, they get to get away from smelly, dirty Runtang for the weekend, and enjoy the countryside. They get to live off us for a couple of days, enjoy our food, drink our booze, and sleep in our beds, and act like they're Gods."

"Yeah and then there's our girl Ellen,'" Smedley chuckled.

"What's that supposed to mean," Ederly asked. He was peeved.

"What do you think it means, Yank?" Smedley sneered.

"I hope it doesn't mean what I think you're implying," Ederly said.

"Use your imagination, my friend," Smedley said. "Beautiful, young girl…horny old man with power."

"You filthy bastard!" Ederly growled. "I should kick your ass, Smedley!"

"Both of you shut up!" Miss Epley cautioned.

"Well, that Marsden guy…he's drooling all over her."

"Yes, he's drooling all over her, but she's hunting him like a cat hunts a mouse, and you know how that turns out, don't you?"

"Yeah…"

"Okay, then, calm down."

At about seven in the evening they stopped for the day and ate dinner.

After dinner the group from Runtang got their suitcases out of the trunk of the Arrow. Miss Epley showed them to the guest rooms up on the second floor, and then she came down to join her crew at the bar. She poured herself a drink.

"See? Like I said, they came prepared to stay for the weekend," she said.

"Yeah," Ederly said, sarcastically "It looks that way."

"Where's Ellen?" Miss Epley asked.

"She's in the kitchen helping Laa clean up the mess they left," Carver said. "Poor Laa..."

"Poor Ellen," Smedley chuckled.

"How far will she take it?" Ederly asked.

"Far enough," Miss Epley said. "And it's not your worry, Ederly, so don't get involved."

Smedley chuckled aside to Miss Epley, "I think our boy here is in love."

Mr. Marsden came out of his room and down the stairs just as Ellen came out of the kitchen. He wore a green silk shirt. It was unbuttoned half way down his hairy chest and bulging stomach to where it was tucked into his tight, white, belted trousers. He wore a black beret on his head, a red scarf around his neck and a pair of Argentine tango shoes on his pudgy, little feet. Ellen met him at the bottom of the stairs.

"Miss Goodstock!" Mr. Marsden said. His voice was weirdly high-pitched and oddly off key. "Shall we dance?"

Miss Epley nodded to Carver and he wound up the Victrola and set the record to spinning. Soon the grainy sounds of a tango wafted out into the air. Mr. Marsden took Ellen's hand and led her to the open space in the great room where they began to dance. Banks, Gilmore, and the two accountants came out of their rooms upstairs. They leaned against the banister and looked down, smiling.

Epley and Smedley did all they could not to laugh. There was Ellen all sweaty in her uniform, fresh out of the kitchen, being jerked about like a puppet on a string by a short, chubby, little man dressed as if he were going to a costume ball. Smedley actually had to bite his lip to keep from bursting into a fit of laughter. Ederly, however, didn't think it was funny at all. He drank three shot glasses full of whiskey, without a pause, one after the other.

Four tangos later and Mr. Marsden led Ellen over to the bar. They were both breathing hard.

"Scotch or whiskey?" Carver asked.

"Whatever," Mr. Marsden said. He panted with his tongue halfway out of his mouth.

Carver poured him a scotch. Ellen fixed herself a bourbon.

"You dance just divinely, Miss. Goodstock," Mr. Marsden said. He took a drink. "Ah…good scotch!"

Ederly could see that Ellen was exhausted. She had just finished helping Laa in the kitchen when Marsden cornered her. She was probably on her way to her room to take a shower, and here she was, trapped. Carver put on another record, this time it was a series of waltzes. Mr. Marsden took a quick sip from his glass and grabbed Ellen's arm and pulled her out to dance again. Ederly could see her forced smile. He watched in agony.

Finally it all came to an end. It was late and they went to bed.

The next day, Saturday, they continued the inventory. That evening, after dinner, Mr. Marsden was back in costume and pulling Ellen all about in a torrid tango again.

By noon Sunday, the inventory was completed. Mr. Marsden held the resulting report in his hand in the great room, as he gave his critique.

"Well, we're finished at last," he said. "It went fairly well, but we did find a few problems. Nothing really major, but still, serious enough. Some wrenches and other tools were found missing from the mechanic's tool sets. The spare tires on one of the small trucks and a jeep were also missing. The jack and the wrench is missing from one of the big trucks. Several spare vehicle batteries, the ones for backup, are missing. The service manuals for the generator and water purification system are missing..." He went on for several more minutes. Things didn't look very good for Virginia Epley. She would have to pay for it all.

At some point, Mr. Marsden paused for effect. He frowned, as if to say, "Naughty...naughty..." Then suddenly he smiled and put the report on the dining table

"Okay, having said all that, here's what's going to happen," Mr. Marsden said in a superior, patronizing voice.

"Runtang is never going to see that report. Why? Because I'm giving you until next year to correct all these discrepancies. As far as Runtang is concerned, everything is fine." Then, "Is that okay with you, Miss Epley?"

"Oh, yes, sir! Thank you, sir!" Miss Epley led the crew in a long round of loud applause. Mr. Marsden took a bow. He was the hero of the day. "Thank you sir!" she repeated, forcing a tortured smile.

"Alright, then," Mr. Marsden said. "This will be our last night here, so let's all enjoy ourselves, shall we?"

"You shitty, little, bureaucratic, son of a bitch!" Miss Epley muttered low, so as not to be heard. For the first time in her life, she felt helpless. She was losing control of her own house, her own people. This paper pusher from headquarters came in here and ordered her around like she was some little piss-ant! The bastard! She glared at him as Mr. Marsden went over to talk to Ellen.

Later, it was the same as the night before, except that the drivers and accountants joined the enclave crew at the bar for drinks and snacks while they watched Mr. Marsden and Ellen dance. Banks invited Miss Epley out onto the floor, but she declined. The dance floor belonged to Mr. Marsden, as he put on a show of his tango skills, using Ellen's body as a prop. As he jerked her about the floor, she held on to keep from slamming into the dining room table. Ederly ground his teeth and tossed down drink after drink.

After the tangos came the waltzes. For half an hour Mr. Marsden and Ellen floated around the floor. He held her very tight. Several times he put his fat, little mouth to her ear and whispered something. Ellen shook her head, as if to say, no. He laughed it off each time. Her face was flushed with anger.

She glanced over at Ederly. Their eyes met briefly and suddenly Ederly was out on the floor.

He grabbed Mr. Marsden's arm, jerked him around, and punched him square in the nose. Ellen gasped and Miss Epley groaned as Mr. Marsden spun completely around and fell backwards, draped over the dining room table, holding his face with both hands. His nose was gushing blood. Everyone crowded around Mr. Marsden, trying to help him.

Miss Epley went over to Ederly. At first he thought she was going kill him, but instead she said, "Nice shot, Yank! Now get the hell out of here! I don't want to see your ass until they're gone!"

"Where should I go?" Ederly asked drunkenly.

"Anyplace! Just get the hell out of here! Go!"

Ederly turned and ran towards the porch, and out into the night.

Smedley watched him go. "We've got our boy now, Virginia," he whispered. "We've got him good!"

8.

It was late Monday morning, and they were all out in the yard standing around the Pierce Arrow. The people from Runtang were all packed and ready to leave. Banks and Gilmore tried to hide their smug grins. They now had a good story to tell back at Headquarters, in Runtang.

"So, he's gone, is he?" Mr. Marsden asked. His nose was bandaged and stuffed with cotton, and he spoke with a nasal tone. He was clearly in pain.

"Yes, sir," Miss Epley said. "He ran off right after he hit you, sir. I don't know when he'll come back."

"Well, I want him sacked, understand? And I'm pressing charge against him for assault and battery. I want to see him in Runtang Prison."

"I understand, sir. And I personally apologized for his bad behavior," Miss Epley said, trying to keep a straight face. She was on the verge of laughing.

Mr. Marsden turned to Ellen. He took her hand. "I will really miss you, my wonderful, Ellen of the tango! I wish I could take you back with me, my dear. We would show those amateurs in Runtang how the tango is really done."

Ellen curtsied. "Thank you, sir."

"If you're ever in Runtang, look me up, young lady. I'll show you the town." Mr. Marsden said.

"Thank you sir, I will."

After they drove away, Miss Epley broke down and laughed so hard she actually went down on her knees, holding onto Smedley for support.

"He isn't all that bad," Ellen said. "He really can dance well, you know?"

"Oh, sure, he was a regular Valentino!" Smedley chuckled.

"Oh, shut up, Smedley!" Ellen suddenly felt neglected. She enjoyed being the center of attention for those three days. "At least he's a gentleman."

"Maybe you should take a hiatus and go to Port Runtang and look him up," Smedley said. "I bet you and his wife and six kids would be very happy together!"

"He doesn't wear a ring," Ellen said. "He's not married."

"I wouldn't count on that," Miss Epley said. "Barnhart doesn't let families come to the island. It's too dangerous. Marsden might have a family back in Hong Kong or London. Who knows?"

"Where's that stupid Yank?" Ellen said. "I hope he gets bit by a snake."

Suddenly they heard a truck door open and shut in the distance. Moments later Ederly, unsteady on his feet, holding his head, and groaning, staggered up from the lower yard.

"Hi," Ederly groaned, "anybody want a hangover?" He walked past them, and staggered up the porch stairs and into the house. They all followed. Once inside, they watched Ederly drag himself up to his room.

They went to the bar and sat down to talk.

"Well, we won't see him for the rest of the day," Smedley said.

"It's just as well," Miss Epley said, "it's too late to go out on a run, anyway."

"And it looks like rain, too," Carver said.

"Don't say it, Carver," Smedley said.

"Don't say what?"

"Don't say it rains on this side of the island, because, blah, blah!" Smedley sneered.

"I wasn't going to say that, Smedley!"

Ellen looked thoughtful. "The Yank is in hot water, isn't he?"

"Yep," Miss Epley said. "But the beauty of that is he's one of us, now."

They all nodded. It was true. Ederly had done a deed foul enough to get him into the club. He was, for all practical purposes, neutralized. He might be called back to Hong Kong any day now and face charges of assault and battery. He was facing two years in prison, at least.

"Let's toast to Ederly," Carver said. They all poured drinks and held their glasses up.

"And may he rot in jail, right Ellen, my love?" Smedley added, chuckling.

Ellen only shrugged. The big man stared, wondering if maybe the Yank hadn't gotten a hold on her.

Virginia Epley pointed a nodded at Ellen. "Tomorrow, while you and the Yank are out on a run, pick his brain. Find out everything you can about him and Barnhart."

Ellen shrugged. "Sure, whatever."

Later that day it began to rain very hard. It sounded like a herd of water buffalo were dancing on the tin roof of the *bahn*. Time moved at a snail's pace. No one felt like playing dominoes or cards or even drinking.

A cool, moist wind blew in through the screened-in porch, bringing with it the smell of growing things. The noise of the rain drowned out the usual jungle sounds. Around midnight, the native in charge of running the generator shut it down for a few hours. By then they were all asleep in their rooms. Before they knew it, dawn arrived, and they were eating a hasty breakfast, and back on the road.

Ellen and Ederly drove out of the enclave, onto the jungle road. The thirst caused by his hangover was still with him. He reached for one of the two water canteens and drank heavily.

"Easy on the water, Ederly," Ellen warned.

"What's the place called, again? I didn't quite catch it." Ederly was still a bit groggy.

"It's called *Bahn-sur-Wan*," Ellen said. "You don't listen very well, do you, Ederly?"

"It all sound the same to me," Ederly muttered.

They drove along the dirt road at a good speed with the windows cranked down to catch any stay breezes, but the cab of the truck was still hot and stuffy. They noticed that the sky was getting a bit grey, and clouds were forming in the distance.

"What if it rains?" Ederly asked.

"Let's hope it doesn't," Ellen said.

"Yes, but if it does?"

"We'll worry about that if and when the time comes."

"Yes, but…"

"It'll be my problem, not yours, so don't worry about it, okay!" Ellen said sharply.

"Sure."

Ederly sat back and listened to the sound the canvas top made as the wind inside the cab pushed up against it. It sounded like a bed sheet flapping on a clothesline. He looked up and saw a spot where it was torn. He reached up and poked his finger into the opening and chuckled.

"Marsden missed one," Ederly said.

"Speaking of Mr. Marsden," Ellen said, "he's going to press charges against you."

"Oh, really?" Ederly chuckled.

"I wouldn't laugh if I were you, Yank. Assault and battery is taken serious around here. It's worth two to three years in jail."

Ederly stared over at Ellen. "You know why I smacked the bum, don't you?"

"I really don't care why you did it."

"Alright then, let not talk about it shall we?"

They drove along in silence. The narrow road wound between lush, green rice paddies where natives looked up and waved at them. After a while they came into a wide-open area of dry, gray, hardpan, where nothing seemed to be able to grow. It was a strange, depressing place, a vast area of nothingness. There wasn't a blade of grass or a palm tree in sight. About halfway through, Ellen pointed to a huge hill of shale rock, off to the left.

"What's that?" Ederly asked.

"Look closely...what do you see?"

Ellen slowed down so Ederly could get a better look at the top of the hill. To him it appeared to be the ruins of an old monastery. It's dark, crumbling walls stood out against the sky and clouds. There was a path going up to it, but there were no people or vehicles around to suggest visitors. A dozen or so huge, black birds, vultures, floated on the rising currents, flying round in circles, above it.

"What is it?"

"It's the ruins of *Wat-seh-Ghow*," Ellen said. "Long ago it was the hideout of an ancient cult that worshiped cobras."

"I don't see anyone there."

"There's a curse on the place. No one goes up there."

The road curved to the left, toward the ruins. The hill which it sat upon grew higher and the ruins seemed to get larger. It looked dreary and deserted, and strange, as if it belonged to another time and place. Finally the road turned to the right, and they left *Wat-seh-Ghow* behind.

91

"What's the story about it?" Ederly asked. "Do you know?"

Ellen nodded. "Yeah. It's said that the cobra cult was immune to cobra bites and would stay that way as long as they sacrificed virgins to the cobra god. So they kidnaped young girls from the villages and threw them into a pit full of cobras to appease him. The members of the cult were invincible. Everybody was afraid of them."

"Well, it looks like they're gone now," Ederly chuckled.

"I wouldn't be too sure," Ellen said. "Every once in a while someone will claim they saw a man change into a cobra or a cobra change into a man. And young girls still come up missing."

"Just stories. Too much of...what do they call that native drink?"

"*Nam-soat.*"

"Yeah, they say it rots the brain."

Ellen chuckled. "Where did you hear that?"

"Back in Runtang, when I arrived," Ederly said. Ellen smiled and drove on.

In about half an hour they came into the village of *Bahn-sur-Wan*. It looked pretty much the same as the other villages they had visited the week before, but they didn't get as much craft wares, and the price had gone up a bit. Still, they got what was there and started back. In all that time they saw only one other truck going in the opposite direction, and hardly any natives. As they came into sight of *Wat-Seh-Ghow*, Ederly stared at it.

"Have you ever been up there?"

"Once. With Smedley and one of the mechanics who work at the enclave. He's from the village we just left. He was our paid guide," Ellen said. "Why? You want to go up there, Yank?"

"I was thinking about it…if we have time?"

"Maybe…if you make it quick," Ellen said.

A little ways on, Ellen turned right onto the hardpan road that led to the base of the ruins. She turned and backed around, pointing the nose of the truck towards the main road. She cut the engine, and reached under her seat and fumbled around for a moment and pulled out an English naval revolver. She laid it across her lap.

93

Ederly chuckled. "Going hunting?"

"Well...there it is, Ederly," Ellen said, ignoring the question. She nodded at the hill. "Have at it, my friend. But make it quick."

Ederly hesitated for a moment. The place suddenly looked ominous.

"Well, yes or no?" Ellen said. "We haven't much time."

Ederly got out and stretched. He saw the worn path, went to it, and started up the rocky incline. It proved hard going from the start, and by midway, he was panting like a dog. He looked up and saw that the sky had darkened. Once he slipped and lost his footing on the loose stone, but managed to stop from rolling down the hill. Soon, below him, the truck looked like a toy.

He went on, and half an hour later he was on the top and staring at the ruins. At that point he had a moment of indecision and considered going back down, but he knew she was watching him, so his pride prevented that. He looked up at the vultures. They looked enormous, and he could hear the rush of their wings as they dipped like dive bombers, swooping close to the top of the ruins.

The lose stones made the walking difficult, but he finally approached an opening in the nearest wall. He hesitated for a moment, and then stepped through it.

Suddenly he was in another world. It was gloomy and damp and had a strange smell. There were many inner walls that led to other chambers. Once his eyes adjusted, he saw that the walls were marked with odd cursive letters and crude drawings, some very old, and others more contemporary. There were colors, too, lots of opposing hues of red and green, as well as sienna and ocher. Some of the drawings were pornographic, and others were sadistic and cruel.

Ederly moved carefully, cursing himself for not bringing a flashlight. He walked slowly through two more chambers until he saw a light. He went towards it, to a large, open area, a sort of courtyard that looked out on the land below. The scene there was beautiful. He could see *Bahn sur Wan*, miles away, a tiny spot in the distance.

He stood there for a short time, then turned and looked about the courtyard. He noticed a round, well-like structure in the center of the place. He went over to look down into it and a horrible stench up drafted into his face. He jumped back and shook his head to get rid of the awful smell. He realized it must have been the cobra pit where they threw the young girls. Something, or someone, had recently been thrown down there.

The stench sickened him. He saw enough, he decided to start back. Suddenly he realized he wasn't sure which entrance he came through. There were four, and they were all in shadows, and to make things worse, he felt as if someone was watching him. He started to panic. Quickly he chose one of the portals and moved towards it.

As he stepped forward, a native, almost naked except for pantaloons, jumped out and blocked his path. The man's eyes were like blazing coals, and he held a rock in his hand. Ederly backed away.

"I'm American," was all he could think of saying. Then, suddenly there were two of them.

"Give me money!" one said in broken English.

"Give me shirt…pants…" the other said, a bit clearer.

Ederly reached into his pocket and pulled out a bunch of American coins, pennies, dimes, and quarters that he carried out of habit. He tossed them on the ground and made a dash for the nearest opening. He could hear them coming behind him. His riding boots gave him no advantage against their naked feet. They came on fast and as he came out on the other side, they were almost upon him.

But suddenly they stopped. Ellen was standing at the top of the hill, pointing her revolver at them. She fired a shot into the wall nearby. The ancient brick shattered and sprayed them with hot shards. His attackers turned and ran back into the ruins.

Ederly and Ellen went down the hill at a fast clip, sometimes sliding on their backsides, dislodging a small avalanche of loose stone. They finally got into the truck. Ellen turned the ignition and nothing happened.

"Damn!" she shouted.

She tried again. The engine coughed, then backfired and died. Ederly could see the two men plunging down the hill towards them. They started to throw rocks. Several bounced off the hood, and one hit the side of his door. Suddenly the engine caught, and the truck began to move. Ellen punched the pedal and they shot out onto the road, leaving a cloud of grey dust behind them.

"That was close," Ederly said. "You saved my butt. Thanks…"

Ellen started to laugh. "You should have seen your face, Ederly! I wish I'd had a camera! You looked absolutely terrified."

"I was," Ederly said. He laughed nervously.

It started to rain and Ellen turned on the windshield wipers and the headlights. They rolled up the cab windows to keep dry, but water came in through the tear in the canvas top. It dripped onto the cab seat, and there was little they could do about it. It began to rain harder. Ellen strained her eyes on the road ahead, but she couldn't see very far. Sometimes she had to slow down, and at other times she had to stop completely to wait for a lull in the rain. It was during one of these stops, that Ellen started to question him about Barnhart.

"So, what did Barnhart say about us?" she asked.

Ederly chuckled. "Barnhart? Are you kidding? I never even saw Barnhart, let alone talk to him."

"But, someone spoke to you about replacing Turner…didn't they?"

"Sure," Ederly said.

"You never saw Barnhart, then?"

"Only certain select people get to see Barnhart. He lives up in the top floor of the Barnhart Building...all by himself. He communicates mostly by phone or memorandum. They say he's a bit eccentric."

Ellen stared at Ederly, trying to detect a sign that he was lying. She saw nothing.

"You're kidding me, aren't you?"

"Look, if you must know, it was my boss Davidson who sent me to find out what happened to Turner. I told him I wasn't the right person. I had a great desk job. Now look where I am! In a big, hot crapper! You can believe that or not, but it's the truth."

Ellen said, "I'll think about it."

"Yeah, you just do that, sweetheart!"

"Oh, getting pissed, are we, Yank?"

"And enough of that 'Yank' stuff. I'm about sick of it!" Ederly said.

Ellen chuckled again.

The rain slacked off a bit. Ellen started the truck moving. She could see pretty well now. They rolled down the window to clear the fog off the inside of the windshield. They were making good time now, and she hit the pedal to get more speed.

"We're getting low on petrol," Ellen said. Ederly could detect the edge in her voice.

"Didn't the mechanics fill it up before we left?"

"It was full when we left. It's the stopping and starting in the rain that did it," Ellen said. Then, "Crap! There's something wrong...the batteries are draining."

"Oh, oh..."

"It must be the generator...it's not charging. The headlights won't last long."

"Will we be able to make it back?"

"Maybe...as long as we don't turn the ignition off it'll keep running until we're empty," Ellen said. "If you know how to pray, Ederly, now would be a good time to do it."

"How far are we from the enclave?" Ederly asked.

"About ten kilometers, or less, I suppose...I'm not sure."

Ederly was just about to say something when it began to rain harder. It was a sudden rush, like the bursting of a dam, a roaring deluge that beat on the canvas above their heads. It fell like rock, pounding on the metal truck hood, splattering back against the windshield. They raised the windows and in a few seconds the glass was clouded up and the cab became a hot box of heat and steam. The windshield wipers were useless.

"We'll have to stop...can't see the damn road!" Ellen yelled. Her voice was almost drowned out by the bellowing howl of the rain.

At that moment they hit something on the road. It was a hard hit that jolted their teeth and brought the truck to an abrupt stop. The engine coughed and backfired twice and then died. Ellen and Ederly looked at each other.

"I'll go see," Ederly said.

"No! Stay here! I'll go!"

"No, I'll go!" Ederly insisted.

"God damn it! I'm in charge here, Yank! You stay put, do you hear me?"

101

Before he could argue, Ellen threw her door open and was outside on the road. The rain started to slack off, and in the fading light of the headlights, Ederly could see that a tree had fallen across the road. He saw Ellen go forward and take a look.

From where he sat, it looked to Ederly like the front wheels were wedged between two branches. He saw Ellen kneel down to check for tire damage, then jump back and catch her breath. She came slowly back to the open door and stood looking at him, clutching her left arm above the elbow.

"I've been bitten by a snake," she said, calmly.

"Oh, God!"

Ederly pulled open the glove compartment and grabbed the snakebite kit and scrambled out of the cab. He ran around the back of the truck, and over to her. She sat on the running board. Her face was white as a sheet.

He knew what to do. He opened the kit, took out the tourniquet, and tied it tight above her elbow to shut off the blood flow. He took an antiseptic pad, and gently and carefully swabbed the wound, talking as he worked.

"The fangs didn't go in, but they did tear the skin a bit. Can't do a cut." Ederly spoke rapidly. "Don't want to force the poison in." He took another antiseptic pad out and wiped the wound lightly again.

Ellen began to shiver. "I'm freezing."

Ederly reached into the cab, under the seat, and got the revolver. He stuck it behind his back, under his belt. He grabbed a canteen and slung it over his shoulder, then got the PRC-6 radio and turned it on. All he got was the crackling sound of static. He called "MAY-DAY!" several time, got no answer, and then tossed it under the cab seat.

"I guess we're on our own, sweetheart!" He picked Ellen up in his arms and started walking around the tree.

The truck headlights were dim but gave out enough light for him to slip down into the water-filled ditch alongside the road. The water was up to his hips, and as he lurched along he felt something slide across his leg. It was the snake. It went on past him. He went around the base of the tree, and up onto the road on the other side. He kept walking and soon the headlights of the truck were only a spot in the distance behind them.

It began to rain harder and their wet clothing got heavier. Ederly had to stop once for a short rest, still holding her in his arms. Her body was burning with fever. He finally got up and went on.

Half an hour on the road, and Ellen said, "Water!" Her voice sounded thick and dry. He stopped and lowered her on one knee and somehow got the canteen open and to her lips. She drank long and hard. When she was finished, they went on, but he had to stop often to give her water. Finally, the canteen was empty.

It got harder now for Ederly to get up on his feet. His legs felt rubbery and he had trouble seeing the road when the rain hit him in the face. He had to shake his head to clear his vision.

At one point he began to stumble, and then he was down on his knees, in the muddy road with, Ellen in his lap. She was trembling and jerking in his arms and she asked for water again. He tilted her head back so that the rain ran onto her parched lips and into her mouth. He tried to get up again, but was too exhausted, so he sat there, in the rain, in the middle of the road, holding her close.

Suddenly Ederly heard someone asking for God's help. It slowly dawned on him who it was. He was surprised because he had never prayed before, never asked God for anything.

And now here he was, sitting in the middle of a muddy road, crying and praying for a miracle.

9.

They were only four miles from the enclave when they were discovered. Miss Epley had sent Smedley and Carver out in one of the small trucks, and they came upon Ederly sitting in the middle of the road, holding Ellen in his arms. He just sat there on the muddy road, drenched, and confused, unable to move, holding her so tight they had to pry her out of his arms. They lifted them both onto the flatbed of the truck and raced back to the house.

They put Ellen to bed and radioed to Runtang for a doctor. Miss Epley stayed by her side. Ederly fell asleep at the bar, with a drink in his hand.

Smedley and Carver took one of the big trucks out with a tow chain. They tied the chain around the trunk of the tree, and pulled it off to one side, and then towed the disabled vehicle back into the yard. It had taken them all night.

It was daylight when they sat exhausted at the bar, next to the snoring Ederly. Miss Epley came down for a drink.

"Should I wake the Yank?" Smedley asked Miss Epley.

"No, take him up to his room and put him to bed, Smed," she said.

Smedley eased his enormous hulk off of the bar stool and grabbed Ederly's arm and walked him up the stairs to his room. A few minutes later he returned.

It began to rain very hard. The wind drove sheets of rain across the enclave yard, and the rain drummed against the tin roof so loud it made it difficult to even talk. Large puddles formed out in the yard. The native workers were nowhere to be seen, huddling somewhere out of sight, trying to keep warm and dry.

It rained and thundered all that day and night, but slacked around dawn. At noon, Banks and Gilmore arrived in the Pierce Arrow with the doctor. Miss Epley took him up to see Ellen while Banks and Gilmore joined Ederly, Carver, and Smedley at the bar for drinks and gossip.

"Did Marsden press charges against the Yank yet, Banks?" Smedley asked. He smiled, as he envisioned the Banri police coming to take the American away to the prison in Runtang.

"Marsden?" Banks said. "That's never going to happen." He and Gilmore chuckled.

"Oh," Carver asked. "Why not?"

"Well, it's like this," Banks said. "The esteemed Mr. Marsden isn't in, shall we say, a vertical position, these days."

"What the hell is that supposed to mean?" Smedley asked.

"Well, to put it delicately, Mr. Marsden was caught in a compromising position."

"Could you come to the point, old chap?" Smedley asked. Ederly looked quietly on, listening with curious interest.

"Go ahead and tell it, Banks," Gilmore said. "I want to see the looks on their faces."

Banks took a drink of whiskey and cleared his throat.

"Well, here's what happened," Banks said, trying to keep a straight face. "One day, over at the Barnhart Company Headquarters office, in Runtang, the husband of Mr. Marsden's secretary, Mrs. Dek-dek, walked unexpectedly into Mr. Marsden's office without knocking. Mr. Dek-dek was looking for his wife. He's a busy man and was behind schedule and was in a hurry. Well, at first it appeared as if there was no one in the office, but Mr. Dek-dek looked around to make sure. That's when he heard heavy breathing in the adjoining room. That's the room where they keep all the inventory records."

"What is Mr. Dek-dek's position in life?" Smedley asked.

"Mr. Dek-dek is a Captain in the Banri Police Department," Gilmore said.

"Oh-my-God!" Carver groaned.

"Go on, Banks," Gilmore urged. "Tell 'em what happened next!"

"Well, apparently Mr. Dek-dek knows his wife's moaning when he hears it, so he busts into the records room with gun in hand and sees Mr. Marsden and his sweet, little wife, doing the nasty!"

"No...really?" Smedley said with a chuckle. "Well, it seems like our Mr. Marsden is one careless chap!"

"Not is...was!" Gilmore corrected, "Mr. Dek-dek shot Mr. Marsden then and there, and took his wife home to their three children."

The enclave crew sat stunned and speechless at the bar. Finally Carver raised his glass. "A toast to Mr. Marsden, a decent fellow, when all is considered."

"A fool who forgot to lock his office door," Smedley added. That got a giggle out of Banks and Gilmore.

"Poor Ellen," Carver said. "This will hit her hard."

"Yes, she took a liking to the fool," Smedley said, laughing. Then, "Well, he did treat her like a lady. I'll give him that." He laughed again.

"Yeah, I'll give him that," Ederly muttered softly.

"Another toast," Smedley added. "To Ederly, the luckiest bastard in the world!"

Carver patted Ederly on the back. The American's response was an indifferent shrug.

The doctor and Miss Epley came out of Ellen's room and down to the bar. He refused a drink and motioned to Banks and Gilmore. They got up from the bar and said good-bye, and the three of them got into the Pierce Arrow and left for Runtang.

By then, Ederly was walking up the stairs. He could hear them laughing as he went up to Ellen's door and knocked. He heard her voice and went in, closing the door behind him. She was sitting in bed reading a book.

"Sit down, Ederly," she said. He took the chair by her bed. "I never got the chance to thank you, so thank you, my friend. The doctor said you saved my life. I'm going to be just fine." Ederly didn't care for the 'my friend' part.

"What are you reading?"

"'The Great Gatsby.'"

"You like it?"

"Very. Somehow he reminds me of you."

"Oh, how so?"

"Well, he's sort of heroic but at the same time pathetic and…"

"And he's in love with a woman who loves him, but not enough to give up her secure life. Yet he's willing to die for her. In the end she betrays him. He dies a tragic death."

"You've read it?"

"Yes. It's one of my favorites."

"Mine, too."

Suddenly Ederly said, "Your friend, Mr. Marsden is dead."

After a quick twitch of surprise, Ellen caught her breath. "I'm sorry to hear that." Then, "How?"

Ederly said, "How he died isn't important…and whatever they say downstairs doesn't matter. All you have to know is that he really liked you and gave you the respect you deserve…like they never did…and never will." Ellen began to sob. "Yes, he's worth crying over…so go ahead and cry, you have a right to."

Ederly got up slowly. He leaned over and softly patted Ellen's shoulder. She put her hand on his hand, and they stared at each other a moment. He kissed her on the forehead, nodded and he went slowly to his room.

Downstairs they were laughing and having a very good time.

10.

In a few days Ellen was back on her feet and they were on the road again. This time Ederly drove the truck and she did the negotiating. They did well, and soon the sheds were full once more.

Then one night it began to rain. It rained all that night and the next morning, and kept on raining for four days without stopping. The yard was a trap of potholes and puddles, and sometimes the generator went down. They sat sweating in the humid darkness, waiting for the native repairman, to get it back on line.

After four days of constant rain, they began to get on each other's nerves. Tempers flared and the *bahn* felt like a prison cell closing in on them. On the seventh day, things began to fall apart.

On that day Smedley had fallen asleep at the dining table while reading a book, his head cradled in his arms. Across the room, at the bar, Ederly and Carver were drinking and playing dominoes.

"I guess I win again," Ederly said. He had won three games in a row.

"You cheated! I saw it!"

Ederly laughed. "You can't cheat at dominoes, Carver. It's impossible."

"You did...and I saw it!" Carver was on the verge of tears.

"Carver, Carver! Come on, now!" Ederly said, as if talking to a little boy.

Carver sighed heavily. "Oh, I'm sorry, Ederly. It's just that we've been cooped up in here like chickens for over a week, now. It's driving me insane."

"Relax, it'll stop soon."

"No, it won't stop. It'll go on and on until it rots my brain and drives me totally insane and I'll want to kill myself, or somebody else!"

"Come on," Ederly said. "Drink up. We'll get drunk."

"No...I've got an awful headache..." Carver pressed his thin fingers against his temples. "My skull is cracking. I need some *ghan-cha*."

"*Ghan-cha*? What the heck is that?"

"It's a plant the natives smoke. It cures everything."

"Is that why you guys go to the village on weekends?"

"That and *nam-soat*."

"*Nam-soat*…it seems I've heard of that." Ederly said.

"Oh, that's the good stuff. It's a sweet, syrupy drink. You should really try it…or maybe not. It's habit forming, like *ghan-cha*. It seems that all the good stuff on this darn island is habit forming. You want to try some?"

"Ah, not really."

"Your loss, old chap. You should really come to the village with us some night. Turner did."

"Oh, really? He went there, did he?"

"Did he? He practically lived in the village. He drove Epley crazy…what with his constant smoking *ghan-cha*, drinking *nam-soat*, and messing with the native girls," Carver said. He paused to reflect. "I kind of think she was afraid of Turner."

"He was a bad boy was he?"

115

"Bad? Christ, that's not the word for it. He was absolutely obnoxious."

Carver yawned and stretched, then shivered. He looked across the room at Smedley. "Look at old Smedley. Off in laa-laa land. Can't have that, you know."

Carver got up from the bar and walked quietly up behind Smedley. He picked up the book Smedley had been reading, and slammed it down hard on the table, then darted up the stairs to his room. Smedley gave a start and lost his balance and fell backwards. When his heavy body hit the floor, he rolled sideways and kicked out. His chair went skittering across the room.

Smedley raised his fist and shook it threateningly at the bedroom landing. "I'll kill you, you skinny little fart!"

Smedley got on his knees, grabbed the table, and got up on his feet. He picked up his book and walked to the bar. He poured a drink and sat down as far away from Ederly as he could and ignored him.

"What are you reading, Smedley?" Ederly asked.

"None of your business, Yank."

"No, I'm serious, what are you reading?"

"I'm serious, too. None of your business."

"Okay, fine," Ederly conceded, "None of my business, then."

There was a moment of strained silence. Smedley looked around. "Where's Ellen?"

"Not my day to watch her," Ederly answered sharply.

"Oh, snooty today, are we, Yank?"

"Don't mess with me, Smedley, I'm not in the mood for your crap."

"Tsk, tsk! Touchy, touchy!"

"Look…"

Ellen suddenly came out of the kitchen. She went over to the bar and poured a drink. Smedley stared at her.

"Been in the kitchen talking to Laa?"

"What's it to you, Smed?"

"Better not let Her Ladyship catch you mixing with the peasants, my dear," Smedley said.

"To hell with Her Ladyship," Ellen said. She took a drink of bourbon. "I've had about enough of her."

"Oh, really, now?"

"Yeah, really now. And I'm fed up with you as well."

"My-oh-my! And Ederly too?"

"Yeah, all of you misogynist pricks! Since you asked, old boy!"

Smedley chuckled and looked at Ederly. "Did you hear that, Yank? You're a misogynist prick!"

Ederly shrugged indifferently. "Yeah, I heard." He took a long drink of whiskey and refilled his glass.

"I guess that means Carver, too," Smedley snickered. "Although I've always thought of dear, old Carver as a little pussy, instead!"

Ellen knocked down her drink and refilled her glass. "Do you know what they do down in the village, Ederly? Smedley, Carver, and Miss Epley?"

Smedley suddenly gave Ellen a cold-as-steel look. "Best be careful what you say, old girl!"

"Oh, is that a threat, Smedley? What? You going to kick my ass, Smed, old chap? Is that what you're going to do?"

"I'm only saying watch what you say, is all."

"Let me guess," Ederly said. "They smoke *ghan-cha*, and drink *nam-sout* and pow-wow with the village chief, right?"

"Sure, but you left one thing out...they have lovers there, too, just like Turner did. They broke Barnhart's first commandment. No playing the nasty with the natives."

Smedley's meaty arm came up and his open palm slapped Ellen across the face, sending her rocking off her stool. Ederly looked surprised for a moment then pulled back and drove his fist into Smedley's stomach. The big man groaned and slid down on his knees, gasping for air, clutching his belly.

Ellen rubbed her cheek and got on balance again and looked at Ederly. "Mind your own business, Yank, I could have handled it myself."

Carver heard the commotion and came out of his room. He saw Smedley and hurried down the stairs and over to the bar. He stood looking down at Smedley.

"Say a little prayer for me while you're down there, Smedley, old boy!" He turned to Ellen. "What the heck is going on, my love? What's he looking for down there?"

119

"His ego, probably," Ellen chuckled. "I think he dropped it."

Smedley, after some effort, got his corpulent frame standing. He leaned on the bar and glared at Ederly.

"I'll get you for that, Yank! And you, too, you bitch! And you, Carver, you bastard! I'm really going to get you. As God is my witness, I'll get all of you!"

Miss Epley came from the radio room. She looked grim. She went to the bar and poured a shot of scotch and slugged it down and poured another one. She looked around at them.

"Playing grab ass, are we?" she said flatly.

"The Yank just kicked Smedley's ass," Ellen said.

Miss Epley stared blankly at Ederly. "How nice. Well then Ederly, I guess that makes you second-in-command, now. Unfortunately, there will be no one left here to command anymore."

"What are you talking about, Virginia?" Smedley asked.

"I'm saying we're done for. Finished. Barnhart is cleaning house. He's shutting down the west enclave until further notice. In case you didn't know, we're the west enclave."

120

There was a deadly silence for a moment.

"We…we're being canned? Terminated?" Smedley's voice was strained."

"It looks that way, Smed."

"But…why?" Carver's voice trembled with uncertainty.

Smedley pointed at Ederly. "Ask the Yank. I bet he knows why. Don't you, you back stabbing rat!"

They all stared at Ederly. He looked down at his drink, avoiding their eyes.

"Well," Miss Epley said, "what have you got to say, Yank?"

"Tell them it's not true, Ederly," Carver pleaded. "Smedley's wrong about you, isn't he? Isn't he?"

Ellen chuckled. "Look at him! I think you pegged him, alright, Smed, old boy. He's a Barnhart informer. Just look at his face! I knew it!"

"Well, Ederly?" Miss Epley asked.

"Some of it is true, but not all of it," Ederly finally said. "Yes, Davidson did send me, on Barnhart's orders, to find out what happened to Turner. Turner was telling everybody that he was poisoned on purpose. He said, 'they poisoned me,' over and over. The question in Hong Kong was, was a crime committed, or was it an accident? Either way, they wanted to keep it quiet and deal with it themselves."

"So, they're waiting for word from you, before they act?"

Ederly nodded. "Once I found out what happened, I was to go down to Runtang and send Hong Kong a report," Ederly said. "It would be in their hands, then."

"But you don't know what happened?" Miss Epley said. "Or do you? Did Ellen tell you?"

"No," Ederly said. "I don't know what happened to Turner. Anyone want to tell me...now?"

"Not on your life," Smedley smirked. "Not on your life, Yank."

Miss Epley sighed. "But you all miss the point here. The enclave is being shut down. Get it, shut down! Nobody said we're being replaced. Closing down operations here is something altogether different. I don't get that part at all!"

"So, what do we do?" Carver asked. "Do we carry on as usual, or what?"

Smedley laughed. "You can, if you want to, old boy, but not me. I've dodged my last snake for that old bastard, Barnhart."

Miss Epley looked around, a sad look on her face. "Ten long years and wham! They shut the door in your face, leaving you hanging in the wind! Why don't they just put a bullet in our heads?"

"What can we do? Where can we go?" Carver whined like a wounded animal. He was about to cry.

Smedley put a comforting hand on Carver's shoulder. "Cheer up, old buddy. Think of it…we're free now, free as a bird."

"But…but what will I do? Where will I go?"

"Don't worry, my friend. Ben Smedley will take care of you. I never desert a pal!" Smedley said. He looked at Miss Epley. "And you know something? Right now, I feel like a party! A big, damn party!"

"You're crazy, Ben," Miss Epley said.

"What's wrong with a party, Virginia? Have Laa cook up a delicious meal! Let's eat, drink, and be merry! Then we'll go say good-bye to our *tee-lats* in the village."

123

"And after that?" Miss Epley asked

"And after that, we'll take a truck," Smedley said, " and drive down to Port Runtang and tell them to shove it all up their arses! We collect our wages and book passage to...to...hell, you name it! We can go anywhere we want!"

"I'd like to see London again," Carver said dreamily. "The snow...singing Christmas carols...and all those holidays we never celebrated here. I've forgotten some of them."

"And Paris is just across the pond from Dover," Smedley said. "And after Paris, we'll go down into Pamplona Spain to see the bull fights!"

Virginia Epley turned to Ellen. "Go have Laa dish up a special spread, babe."

"That's the spirit, Virginia," Smedley said. "We'll give ourselves a proper send off, and then get the hell out of here. Leave it all to the Yank, here. He deserves it."

They all laughed. Ellen went into the kitchen to tell Laa.

Suddenly Ederly felt very cold and alone.

11.

After they had all eaten, Ederly joined them in a farewell drink, and then another and another. Finally he lost count and decided that he needed a nap and collapsed over the bar. The last thing he remembered was hearing them come down the stairs with their bags packed. Someone patted him on the back and said something about good luck Yank, and then he heard the sound a truck leaving the compound.

It was still dark outside and close to dawn when Ellen came down from her room. She went over to Ederly and stroked his hair.

"Are you alright, Ederly?" she asked.

He sat up slowly and stretched. "Yes. You're here? You didn't go?"

"No."

"Why are you still here?"

"I wanted to talk to you alone," Ellen said. Then, "Are you still drunk?"

125

"A little, maybe…but I'm okay." He looked around. "Are they gone?"

"Yes, they should be on their way to Runtang by now."

"It's too quiet here."

"Yes, but I can feel their spirits all around us."

Ederly nodded. "Yeah, their ghosts will haunt this place forever." He yawned. Then, "What did you want to talk to me about?"

Ellen sat close to Ederly at the bar. "I wanted to tell you about Turner."

"Okay, I'm listening," he said eagerly, staring at her.

Ellen started with, "When Turner first came here last year he seemed like a nice enough chap. He told jokes and made us laugh and, well…we liked him…and he was well liked by the natives, too. He was sort of clownish so they called him, '*bah-bah-baw-baw*.'"

"What's that mean?"

"Well, it means, 'nutty,' but in a nice sort of way. Turner was very funny. At first he spent a little of his free time down in the village, but then, more and more. He would

126

come back from a run, and then head straight down there. Sometimes we wouldn't even see him until morning, drunk and doped up, unable to do his job. He would just go right to bed."

"How did Epley handle that?"

"They finally had a big fight. Turner would be good for a week, then go right back to his old ways. Things got worse. He got weird on us. His whole personality changed. He got into fights with the native men in the village. It got so bad Carver and Smedley refused to work with him. And so did I. The village chief asked Epley to do something about him. When she confronted Turner, he pulled a carte blanche out and showed it to her."

"A carte blanche?"

"Yes, from Barnhart."

"Turner had a letter of authority from Barnhart himself?"

"Yes. Turner said he was sent personally by Barnhart himself to get the goods on Epley, Carver, and Smedley, for misconduct with the natives. He gave Virginia two choices. Leave him alone and things would be just fine. If not..."

"…then he would spill the beans to Barnhart?"

"Yes."

"That's blackmail!"

"Yes, blackmail," Ellen said. "Virginia couldn't do much except let him have his way. Sometimes he would go out on a run with me. It was hell. I told Virginia I couldn't take it anymore, so she stuck him with Carver. After that he came at me during the night, trying to get into my room, drunk and drugged out of his mind. Once Smedley and he almost got into a fight, but Epley called Smedley off. She was afraid of Turner."

"No wonder someone poisoned the bastard! He deserved it!" Ederly said. Then, "Ah, was it Miss Epley?"

"No."

"Smedley! I knew it!"

"No."

"Not Carver!" Ederly said.

"No, Carver wouldn't hurt a flea."

"Then, it was accidental?"

"No. He…he was poisoned on purpose."

"Who did it?" Ederly dreaded the answer.

Ellen stared at him for a moment. "It was Laa...but I helped her," she said.

Ederly was stunned into silence. "How...why?" he finally asked.

"One night, it was a weekend, I heard voices down in the kitchen. I thought Epley, Carver, and Smedley had come back from the village, but no. it was Turner. I heard his voice. He talked loudly when he was drunk. Then I heard Laa's voice, and. I wondered what she was doing back in the kitchen so late. I listened. They were arguing about something, and Turner was yelling at her. I put on my robe and went down into the kitchen as fast as I could. Turner could get rough, when he drank."

Ellen stopped. Ederly put a hand on her arm. "You want something to drink?"

Ellen shook her head and continued the story. "Turner had been drinking in the village and decided to go over to Laa's *bahn* to mess around with her fourteen year old daughter. When Laa's crippled husband tried to stop him, Turner beat the poor man up and left."

"And Laa followed him back here?"

"Yes, cursing him all the way. She was going to fight him. She went at him with everything she had in her little, eighty-five pound body. Turner slapped her down like she was a fly. When he saw me, his eyes got a crazy look in them. I knew right then that I was in for it! He came at me! Oh, God!"

Ellen started to sob and shake. She stopped to collect her thoughts. Ederly caressed her shoulder.

"Go on."

"I didn't struggle, he was too strong for that. I knew I was really in a tight spot. Best to play him along, wait for an opening, and get out of it. We were the only ones in the house. I ran into the dining room…to the bar..." She paused.

"Go on."

"I poured us both a drink, then tossed mine in his face and ran for the kitchen. He caught me there and I slapped him and he laughed and sat down, pulling me onto his lap. He was in no hurry. He'd torn my robe half off. I told him he'd have to buy me a new one. He kept laughing his silly laugh. He noticed Laa was gone, and he called for her. She was standing in a corner crying and glaring at him. He said he was hungry and yelled at her to go into the larder and get his favorite snack."

"Sardines?"

"Yes. In the short time Laa was gone, he had ripped my robe down to my waist. Laa came back and quickly opened the can of sardines and put them on a pretty plate and on the table so he could see them. He told me to feed him, and I did."

"You don't have to say anymore!"

"I fed him those rancid sardines on that pretty plate while he put his hands all over me and laughed. He was having the time of his life, he was!" Ellen's voice grew louder and more emotional. "Poor Laa! Her pretty face was all bruised and swollen where he had hit her, and her mouth was split and bleeding. Oh, God! Poor, little Laa!"

"Don't!"

"One by one I stuffed those sardines into his mouth, every single one of them*! Eat, you son of a bitch, eat*!" Ellen face was intense. She paused as if to replay the scene in her mind. "When he had finished them all, he yawned. His eyes

131

went all misty and he seemed to lose interest in me. I got up and took Laa home."

"And, after that?"

"When I got back Turner was slumped over the table, mumbling and snoring. I went up to bed and washed my mouth out and took a shower to get the stink of him off me."

"How did it end?"

"In the morning I heard Carver scream, so I dressed slowly and went down there. Turner was in bad shape. He had soiled himself and he was throwing up. He was half-blind. They wrapped him in a blanket and put him in the back of a truck. Carver and Smedley took him to Port Runtang."

"And that was the end of it?"

"Well, Epley found the sardine can. It had a big bulge in it. The sardines were plainly spoiled. I didn't tell her what happened, and Laa never said a word about how she got beaten up. A few days later Epley found my torn robe and noticed the bruises on my neck. Between that and Laa's face, she soon figure it out. They all did. Everything was fine until…"

"Until?"

"Until Turner blabbed in the hospital in Hong Kong. And then you came."

Ederly chuckled. "This is like a crime novel, 'Death by Sardines.'"

"It's no joke."

"Yes, you're right. But anyway, case closed, mystery solved."

"You can make out your report now," Ellen said."

Ederly shrugged. He wasn't enthusiastic. "Report? Oh, yeah, the report."

"So, what will you tell them?"

"I'm not sure. It didn't turn out the way I was hoping," Ederly said.

"What was that?"

"That it was just an accident."

"Well, it wasn't. I fed Turner food that I knew would kill him, and I did it willingly and I'm glad I did it," Ellen said forcefully.

She got up and walked over to the open doorway facing the screened-in porch. A cool gust of sweet, clean, jungle air wrap itself around her. Ederly came up close behind her, almost touching her.

"Look, I'm in a bind here. I'm in love with you."

"I feel sorry for you, then. It won't work out, Ederly." She stepped close to the screen, touching it with one hand. "Another time...another place, maybe...but not here, and not now."

She began to sob. Ederly grabbed her shoulders and turned her gently around and put his arms around her. He kissed her softly. They stood together a long time.

Somewhere a rooster announced the coming of dawn.

12.

Laa came in the morning at her usual time. Ellen joined her in the kitchen while Ederly was upstairs shaving.

The delicate, little woman knew that the crew had left and the enclave was going to be shut down because Epley, Carver, and Smedley had spent the night in the village eating, talking, and drinking with their close native companions. After celebrating, they said their farewells. Just before dawn, they got into their truck and left on the road to Runtang.

"You should come every day as usual anyway," Ellen told Laa, "until they close the *bahn*."

"Oh," Laa said in her lyrical, broken English, "they no close *bahn. Bahn* stay open. It never close."

Ellen smiled. "You don't understand. I have to go. Ederly has to go. No one will be here."

Suddenly they heard the sound of a vehicle in the distance just as Ederly came downstairs into the great room. Ellen came from the kitchen and joined him.

135

"It must be Banks and Gilmore," Ellen said.

"They'll probably shut the house down and take us back."

"It's not that simple. There's a lot of valuable equipment here that has to be taken back to Runtang," Ellen explained, "and somebody has to stay here until it's all removed."

"How long will that take?" Ederly asked.

"Maybe one or two weeks. It all depends. It could be done in a few days, if they send enough drivers up, all at one time."

"The mechanics are probably wondering what's going on," Ederly said.

"Nope. They know. Word travels fast in the village."

The sound was closer now. It wasn't a truck. It turned into the enclave and stopped in the yard. They heard the doors open and close, then the voices of Gilmore and Banks, and a third person. In a few moments the voices were in the kitchen, talking with Laa. Ellen and Ederly could hear someone telling Banks and Gilmore to stay there and eat.

They heard footsteps and suddenly a very old, handsome, intelligent looking, silver-haired man dressed immaculately in tropical whites and matching loafers, and using a cane, came into the great room.

He stopped to stare at Ellen and Ederly.

"I'm Edward Barnhart," he said. "I own this place, and I'm so hungry I could eat a dead skunk!"

For a moment they were stunned. Ellen quickly recovered and said, "I'll tell Laa, sir."

"Too late. I already told her. Who are you, anyway?" He came in close to look at Ellen's face.

"Ellen, Ellen Goodstock, sir," Ellen said. "And he…"

"I know who he is. But for the life of me I don't know why we hired him. He was useless in Hong Kong, and he's useless here. Right, Mr. Ederly?"

Ederly didn't know what to say. "Ah…yes sir. If you say so, sir."

"Well, I do say so, and that's that! So don't argue about it!"

"No, sir."

"Is that all you can say, yes, sir, and, no sir?"

"Yes, sir, I mean, no sir."

"Well, you'd best shut up. I like you better when you shut up. In Hong Kong you didn't say anything. In fact, you never did anything. You were worthless."

The old man sat down at the table. There was a moment of silence.

"Well, isn't anyone going to ask me why I'm here?"

"Why are you here, sir?" Ederly asked.

"Suppose you tell me, Mr. Ederly."

"Well, ah…"

Ellen cut him off. "You're here to sack us and shut the enclave down, right?"

Barnhart chuckled. "Exactly! She's smarter than you are, Ederly! You should ask her to marry you."

"I'm considering that, sir."

"And if she's got any brains, she'll tell you to go climb a tree! You're no prize, you know." He looked over at Ellen. "Goodstock? What a silly name."

"Barnhart is no prize winner, either," Ellen said.

"Oh, spunky, huh? Barnhart smiled. "Well, I like that. I like my women sexy, smart, and spunky."

Ederly cleared his throat. "So, ah, what brings you here, sir?"

"She just told you. To close this evil place down. And have it exorcised by a bishop or somebody. Or something like that."

Ellen said, "You won't be firing just us, you know?"

"Oh? Who else, Miss Smarty Pants?"

"There's Laa, the cook, and the mechanics, and men who work out in the yard. They all have families. And there are the villagers who depend on us to buy their stuff. You'll be hurting lots of people, including yourself."

"So, you think these savages are people, do you?"

"They're not savages, sir. They're good, smart people."

The old man chuckled again. "Now I'm positive you should marry her, Ederly. She has empathy. I like people who have empathy."

"Sir," Ederly said, "about Turner, there is something you should know about him."

Barnhart cleared his throat, and took a deep breath. "Turner? Oh, yes, Turner."

139

"I'd like to tell you what happened here."

Barnhart cut Ederly off with a wave of his cane.

"Before you start blabbing your mouth off, let me say something about Tuner." Barnhart paused and looked at them both. "Do I have your full attention?" They nodded. "Good. Now, about Turner…after he died, we naturally went searching for his next of kin, a wife or mother and father, or children…anybody." Barnhart paused again. "Well, it didn't take long before what we got back was a wanted poster."

Ellen and Ederly both said, "A wanted poster?"

"Yes, a wanted poster. It seems that Turner was wanted in Iowa."

"In Iowa?" Ederly asked.

"Yes, and don't repeat everything I say, Ederly. You're beginning to sound like a parrot." Barnhart stopped again for a second, to yawn. "Where was I? Oh, yes. It appears Turner murdered his wife there, in Iowa, on a farm, and went off leaving three small children all by themselves."

"Jesus!" Ellen muttered.

"Watch your mouth, young lady! I used to be a preacher once, you know! I'll have no blasphemy here!"

140

"Oh, no sir," Ellen smirked, "we don't want any of that now, do we?"

Barnhart's stare turned icy cold. "Are you mocking me, young lady? You're not very wise, you know. And neither are your friends, that Carver and Smedley and that woman, Epley! They won't get away, you know?"

"What do you mean, they won't get away?"

Ederly said, "Ellen! Be careful!"

"Like hell, I'll be careful! I'm not afraid of this old fart!" Then, "What do you mean, they won't get away?"

"The Banri police are waiting for them down in Port Runtang. They'll be charged there, under native law, for moral crimes against the natives. Before he died, Turner told the whole, sordid story. Your friends were unrepentant sinners, plain and simple."

"Who is going to press charges? Not the natives. They won't testify against them," Ellen said.

"You forget one thing, Miss Goodstock, I own this island. And your friends will be charged, unless…"

"Unless what?"

141

"Unless you and Ederly here agree to a proposition of mine."

"A proposition?" Ederly asked.

"Yes. Why do you think I came all the way from Hong Kong? To see you're ugly face?"

"Wait a minute," Ellen said. "If we agree to your proposition, will you lay off Epley, Carver, and Smedley?"

The old man nodded. "I will. You have my word."

"Okay…what's the proposition?" Ellen asked.

"I want to reopen the west enclave as a tourist stop. You two will run it."

"A tourist stop?" Ederly asked.

"There you go again, Ederly, repeating everything I say," Barnhart said. "Yes, a bed and breakfast for tourists. I'm setting up a tourist bureau in Runtang. We'll have guided tours to the ruins of that old monastery, as well as tours of the villages that make the artifacts. There are lots of sights to see on Banri. I've already started construction on a hotel in Runtang. Guided tours will start from there and go all over the island."

"But what about the cottage industry? The craft ware business?"

"Oh, we'll run that straight from Runtang. It's easier and cheaper that way. No middle man."

"So, you're turning all the other enclaves into bed and breakfast places, too?" Ellen asked.

"That's right, all of them...east, north, and south," Barnhart said. "So, are you two in or not? If not say so. I'll hire somebody else."

"I'm in," Ellen said without hesitation. "How about you, Ederly?"

"Absolutely," Ederly said. 'If, you'll marry me?"

Ellen looked at old Barnhart. "What do you think? Should I?"

"That was the second part of my proposition...only married couples need apply," Barnhart said. "So, yes, marry him, or somebody else, if you want to. I don't care."

Ellen turned to Ederly. "Okay, Yank, I'll marry you."

Ederly took Ellen in his arms and kissed her. It was a long kiss.

"Stop that," Barnhart said. "I haven't had my breakfast yet."

Ellen broke the embrace. "I'll go help Laa with breakfast."

"Two eggs, over easy, toast, marmalade, and Jasmine tea, thank you," Barnhart said.

Suddenly the old patriarch slumped back in his chair, his head down on his chest. Ellen looked on in horror. She put a hand over her mouth and pointed.

"My God! He just died," she gasped. Suddenly they heard a snore.

"No, he's sleeping," Ederly chuckled. Ellen sighed a sigh of relief.

"I'll go help Laa with breakfast. You watch that he doesn't fall over and break his neck, or we'll be out of a job."

Ellen started for the kitchen, then stopped and turned to face Ederly.

"I want a proper proposal and a ring, Yank, or the deal is off on the marriage part."

"Sure," Ederly said, "and maybe Barnhart will be best man."

"God help us!" Ellen Goodstock turned and went into the kitchen laughing

"See, *Khune* Ellen? *Bahn* no close," the little woman said. Ellen gave her a big hug.

The End.

About the Author

R. Annan

R. Annan is a seasoned and traveled author with many interests. As a career serviceman he served in Korea and Vietnam. He also completed a one-year course at the Defense Language Institute at Monterey, California, and graduated from the University of South Florida with a B.A. in Art and Art History. After taking a two-year course in screenwriting at the Hollywood Scriptwriting Institute, he established *The Old Time Radio Club Time Machine* as both a scriptwriter and an actor.

He currently has many short novels in the works: *Mr. Dobbs: A Christmas Ghost Story*; *The Ghost of Reginald Burton, Esquire; Vzor's Prisoner: A Sci-fi Novel; Elke: A Love Story; The Princess of Ovaar: A Sci-fi Fantasy; Gemma's Angel; Sen Loi and The Debutante of Kowloon; The Fight for the Lazy M: A Western;* and *From This Valley: A Korean War Story*. Look for these books to appear soon.

A Note from the Author

If you've enjoyed this book, would you consider rating it and reviewing it? Thank you!